"You cheated on our bargain."

Drake's eyes burned into her as he continued. "You believed that if you weren't employed by the studio I wouldn't publish the photographs you agreed to pose for."

"You can humiliate me as much as you care to," Emma stormed, trying to ignore the vulnerability he revealed in her. "But not Emma Court— newscaster! I won't be used in your publicity war against a rival."

"You surprise me, you know." He was watching her closely, reassessing her. "It's very strong, isn't it, this code of ethics of yours? First it led you into protecting your sister and then your would-be employers." He paused, as if considering an idea. "I wonder if it could be extended to me, as well."

"You?" Emma's shock was genuine. "What would you need to be protected from?"

PENNY JORDAN was constantly in trouble in school because of her inability to stop daydreaming—especially during French lessons. In her teens she was an avid romance reader, although it didn't occur to her to try writing one herself until she was older. "My first half-dozen attempts ended up ingloriously," she remembers, "but I persevered, and one manuscript was finished." She plucked up the courage to send it to a publisher, convinced her book would be rejected. It wasn't—and the rest is history! Penny is married and lives in Cheshire.

Books by Penny Jordan

HARLEQUIN PRESENTS
746—DARKER SIDE OF DESIRE
755—RULES OF THE GAME
761—CAMPAIGN FOR LOVING
770—WHAT YOU MADE ME
785—THE ONLY ONE
794—THE FRIENDSHIP BARRIER
809—THE SIX-MONTH MARRIAGE
818—TAKEN OVER
826—TIME FUSE
833—YOU OWE ME
850—EXORCISM
868—PERMISSION TO LOVE
883—INJURED INNOCENT
897—THE HARD MAN

HARLEQUIN SIGNATURE EDITION
LOVE'S CHOICES

PENNY JORDAN

fire with fire

Harlequin Books

TORONTO • NEW YORK • LONDON
AMSTERDAM • PARIS • SYDNEY • HAMBURG
STOCKHOLM • ATHENS • TOKYO • MILAN

Harlequin Presents first edition September 1986
ISBN 0-373-10916-4

Original hardcover edition published in 1985
by Mills & Boon Limited

CHAPTER ONE

WHEN the central heating boiler had refused to reignite despite all her efforts Emma sat back on her heels and scowled ferociously at it. They really ought to have a new one, but her father's income as vicar of a small country parish did not run to such self-indulgences.

Sighing, she pushed her hair back out of her eyes. Thick and curly, its dark chestnut colour was a striking foil for her creamy skin and widely spaced cool grey eyes, their coolness masking an intelligence and humour only perceived by the most discerning observer.

'Emma. Oh thank God you're here. You must help me, I'm in the most awful mess.'

It was far from being the first time Emma had heard those words on her younger sister's lips, and she didn't pay too much attention at first, her brain still trying to resolve the problem of the central heating boiler, but when Camilla burst into tears and gulped hysterically about 'going to prison' and 'losing David', she realised that whatever the 'mess' that she was in, it was something more serious than her usual small traumas.

Petite and blonde, Camilla had a way of attracting trouble that was completely at odds with her delicate appearance. The trouble was that her fairy prettiness had meant that her sister had been petted and spoiled almost from the moment of her birth, Emma reflected, brushing the dust off her hands and getting to her feet.

'Come on Cammy,' she began bracingly, 'whatever it is it can't be as bad as all that ... David adores you ...'

'Don't call me "Cammy",' came the tearful response. 'You know David doesn't like it ... and it *is* bad Emma, just as bad as it could be ...'

More tears flowed.

'Well then you'd better tell me all about it.' Calmly pulling out two chairs from the wooden kitchen table, Emma sat down in one and waited for Camilla to settle herself in the other. The trouble was that as their mother had died when Emma was ten and Camilla barely six, she had somehow taken over the role of mothering and protecting her younger sister and Camilla had grown used to expecting Emma to resolve all her life's crises for her. What on earth could it be this time? Probably a quarrel with David's mother over arrangements for the wedding, Emma thought wryly. Since she had become engaged to David Turner, the highly-strung Camilla had seemed to mature a little, but with the wedding approaching fast her tearful outbursts had become more and more common. A frown creased Emma's forehead. There were times when she wondered if her younger sister actually wanted to marry David. They had known him for most of their lives and while she liked him, Emma couldn't blind herself to the fact that he was very much under his mother's thumb, and that if Camilla wanted a happy and smooth married life she would have to learn to get on better with her prospective mother-in-law than she did at the moment.

The main problem was that at heart Mrs Turner was an arrogant snob. Her husband had been extremely wealthy and they had moved to the village when David was four and Emma the same age. Emma suspected that the only reason they had been admitted to David's group of friends was because of their father's family connections—his uncle had been a colonel in one of the better regiments and had married the daughter of a baronet.

It didn't seem to matter to Mrs Turner that the vicar and his wife had very little contact with these minor relations; their existence was sufficient to make his children acceptable playmates for her son. But that had been twenty years ago. She was not as keen to welcome one of the vicar's daughters as her daughter-in-law as she had been as 'friends' of her son. The Turners were comparatively wealthy. They owned the largest house in the district and Mrs Turner rather liked to play 'Lady Bountiful'. The village fête was always held in the grounds of the Manor and Mrs Turner liked it to be known that she was heavily involved in several prestigious charities. Emma didn't much like her, but Camilla was marrying her son, and the fact that David was dominated by his mother was something she was going to have to accept.

Mrs Turner never lost an opportunity of pointing out that David could have done much better for himself. In Camilla's place Emma doubted that she could have stomached it, but Camilla claimed that she loved David and that he loved her, and that together they would be strong enough to withstand Mrs Turner's acid barbs.

Privately Emma doubted it. Beautiful though
Camilla was, like David she was inclined always to
look for the easiest route through life. If David had
not been an extremely wealthy young man Emma
doubted if Camilla would have looked twice at him.
Camilla had always deplored the poverty that went
with their father's vocation; as a teenager she had
never ceased bemoaning the lack of material assets
when compared to those of her friends; the problem
was that because of her blonde prettiness she had
been petted and spoiled—friends' parents had
included her on various holiday treats; their father
had always been coaxed to find from somewhere the
extra pennies needed for new clothes ... Not that
Emma begrudged her any of it—no, in character as
well as looks they were completely dissimilar. From
being a young teenager Emma had known what she
wanted from life and it hadn't been marriage to a
man like David.

Now, she was poised on the brink of taking the
all important step forward in her new career. After
leaving college she had been lucky enough to get a
job with their local radio station; from there she
had progressed to regional television and now her
current boss had advised her of a plum job coming
up with one of the National networks, which he
thought she stood a good chance of getting.

At present she was a co-presenter on an early
news local programme, but she had been doing the
job for several years and was ready for something
else. Her goal was a top newsreading or anchorwoman job; perhaps if she was very, very lucky,
even something on breakfast television, but she
had a long way to go before reaching that
objective she reminded herself.

However, the interview her boss had lined up for this new National job sounded extremely promising. She wouldn't be the only one going after it, but Robert Evans considered that she had a more than fair chance.

'You've got the looks,' he had told her only this morning, 'and the brains. And let's not disillusion ourselves, you need both, unfair though that sounds.'

Emma hadn't disputed it. It was an unfair fact of life that while male presenters were chosen on ability and personality alone, female ones needed to have an acceptably attractive face and figure. Although nowhere near as pretty as her younger sister, Emma knew she was reasonably attractive. Her bone structure was good, her figure elegantly slender. Her air of cool self-containment put a lot of men off, she knew, David in particular . . . she frowned a little remembering Mrs Turner's latest broadside. She had called round the day after the local newspaper had carried a small article mentioning the fact that Emma was being considered for a top London job.

Being in television was all very well in its way, she had begun when Emma asked her in, 'but it wasn't really the sort of thing David wanted to be connected with. Reading the news was all very well . . . but it could lead to other things. . .'

Anyone would have thought she was proposing to pose nude for a Page 3 photograph, Emma thought sardonically. She knew that Mrs Turner was being ridiculous and so she suspected did the older woman, but David took his mother's every word seriously and she had boiled with angry indignation at the suggestion that her job somehow made Camilla unfit to become David's wife.

Camilla was twenty-two years old and should be able to cope with her own problems, she knew, but she didn't have the heart to tell her so, saying instead, 'Come on then, what's it all about.'

'Do you remember last month when I went to stay with Fiona?'

Emma nodded. Fiona Blake was one of Camilla's old schoolfriends. At the moment she was flat-sharing in London with two other girls while she tried her hand at modelling. Fiona's parents were wealthy enough for it not to matter whether Fiona made a success of her 'career' or not, and privately Emma did not think she would.

'Well while I was there Fiona took me to this party. I didn't want to go, but she insisted.'

Listening to the aggrieved note in her sister's voice Emma sighed. Nothing that went wrong in her life was ever Camilla's fault; she had always been victimised by someone else.

'Fiona wanted to go because the party was being held by Drake Harwood . . .'

Drake Harwood? The name was familiar, as well it might be Emma thought, recollecting how the first time she had heard it it had conjured up visions of a tough, buccaneering individual. He was an up and coming entrepreneur who had recently bought out Scanda Enterprises and he was reputed to be extremely wealthy.

'Fiona wanted to go because he's taken over *Macho* magazine, and she thought she might be able to persuade him to use her as one of his models.'

'*Macho*? Fiona wants to appear in that?' Emma

grimaced distastefully. 'Honestly Camilla that girl has more hair than wit. What on earth would her parents say? It's a girlie mag isn't it?'

'Fiona says it's the only way for unknowns to break into modelling these days.' Camilla defended her friend. 'She says. . .'

'Never mind what she says,' Emma broke in, 'Just tell me what's got you in such a state. He didn't ask you to pose for him did he?' she guessed, darting a frowning look at her sister. Despite her plans to marry David Camilla had always had a yen for the glamour of a 'Hollywood' type existence. It was just as well she lacked the ambition to do anything other than daydream about it, Emma decided, hiding her relief at Camilla's vigorous shake of her head. Camilla simply did not have the determination to succeed in such a dangerous world.

'No . . . no . . . nothing like that.' She bit her lip. 'Promise you won't be cross, and that you won't breathe a word to David. He'll never marry me if he finds out.'

'Good heavens, what on earth have you done?' She asked it light-heartedly not wanting Camilla to see her concern. Snippets of gossip she had heard and read about Drake Harwood were coming back to her. He had made it the hard way, grafting for every penny of the first few thousand pounds he made; working on a building site until he had enough to start up his own contracting firm. From then on he had gradually built up his empire until now at thirty-four he was considered one of the shrewdest and most dangerous businessmen around.

Macho magazine was just a small part of that

empire, she recollected, something he had acquired when he took over Scanda Enterprises. She recollected reading somewhere that it had a pretty poor circulation and that he had been challenged by a rival magazine owner to beat their figures.

No doubt the whole thing was simply a publicity ploy she reflected cynically, certainly the supposed 'rivalry' had gained them both a good deal of newspaper space, but how much of an interest he intended to take in what was only a small part of his empire she didn't really know. Certainly if he intended to use girls like Fiona as his models he wouldn't do much to improve circulation.

'So, you went to this party with Fiona,' Emma pressed, 'and. . .'

'And I don't remember anything else until the next morning,' Camilla gulped tearfully, 'when I woke up in a strange bedroom and . . .'

'An even stranger man in bed beside you?' Emma supplemented drily. 'Mrs Turner's going to love that.'

'No . . . no I was in bed on my own . . . in a room of my own,' Camilla protested. 'I must have had too much to drink . . . either that or there was something in them, but Emma, I was so frightened . . . I just had to get out of that house . . . I kept thinking what if David could see me now, so . . .'

'So . . .' Emma prompted.

'Well, I was still fully dressed, so I just got up and went downstairs. There was no one about, but there was a car outside—a red Ferrari, and the keys were in it . . . so I . . . I took it. . .'

'You did what?' Emma stared at her. 'But Camilla you don't drive. You've always hated it . . . you don't have a licence . . .'

'I know, but I was so terrified of being found there . . . I daren't ring for a taxi . . . I had to leave . . . and I do know how to drive . . . but the car was so big . . .'

Closing her eyes Emma forced herself not to interrupt.

'Don't tell me,' she said at last. 'You hit something?'

'A stone bollard,' Camilla admitted. 'You see it was very early in the morning—there wasn't any traffic, but I saw this milk cart coming and I panicked. I hit the kerb and then this bollard . . .'

'And . . .?'

'I just got out and ran. Eventually I found a taxi, and I went back to the flat . . . Fiona wasn't there, but when she came in I told her what had happened, and she told Drake Harwood, and he's threatening to sue me for stealing his car and smashing it up . . .'

Fresh tears started to fall. 'It will be in all the papers and everyone will know I spent the night there. David will find out and he'll never marry me . . . His mother wouldn't let him.'

Emma suspected that she was right. She gnawed thoughtfully on her lower lip, silently condemning both her sister and Fiona as a pair of stupid fools.

'Haven't you been to see Drake Harwood, and tried to explain? I'm sure if you told him the full story . . .'

Camilla shuddered. 'You haven't met him. He's dreadful . . . So uncouth. Fiona thinks he's exciting . . . but I didn't like him. I couldn't go and see him Emma, I just couldn't . . . but his solicitor has already written to me. He wants me to pay for the damage to his car, otherwise he's going to sue . . . and I can't afford it.'

'So what do you want me to do about it,' Emma asked, already mentally bowing to the inevitable.

Tears were transformed into a radiant smile as Camilla turned towards her. 'Oh Emma, I was hoping you would help me. Couldn't you go and see him . . . Explain . . .'

'Explain what?' Emma asked drily. 'That you don't want your mother-in-law to know that you spent the night in one of his beds and then stole his car. . . . And what about paying for the damage Camilla?'

'He doesn't need the money, he's filthy rich,' Camilla said sulkily, 'he's just doing this because I wouldn't pay any attention to him . . .'

'Ah . . . You mean he fancied you and you gave him the cold shoulder? Umm, I can see that in those circumstances he might not be prepared to let you off the hook so lightly.'

'But you will try and do something . . . you will go and see him?' Camilla pleaded. 'There's still a month to go to the wedding and this letter says if I don't pay for the damage within seven days, legal action will be taken.'

The man could always simply be trying it on, Emma thought, but then given his reputation and his tough upbringing it might not be wise to assume so. 'Camilla are you sure this marriage to David is what you really want,' she asked slowly. 'You know you ought to be able to tell him about this, to . . .'

'To ask him for several thousand pounds, a month before we get married?' Camilla asked bitterly. 'Yes I could tell David, Emma, but he would tell his mother and I could just imagine her reaction. You know she doesn't want him to marry me, and yes, I do want to marry him. Can't you see, I'm not like you, I don't want a career or to be independent. I just want to live quietly and comfortably. . .'

The accent probably being on the latter, Emma thought drily, but refrained from saying so. 'Let me look at the letter,' she requested.

She read it quickly, sifting through the legal verbiage to the nitty-gritty, and when she had done so, she could see why Camilla was in such a panic. Drake Harwood wanted and intended to have his pound of flesh. Well she would just have to try and find some means of persuading him otherwise.

'You won't tell him the truth will you?' Camilla begged. 'I wouldn't put it past him to tell one of his newspaper friends and then it will be all over the papers.'

'I hardly think the fact of your crashing his car merits such coverage Camilla,' Emma told her mildly. 'You're getting things a little out of perspective.'

'You don't know how furious he was about his car.' She shuddered. 'Fiona says he had only just bought it . . . *You* haven't met him Emma. You don't know what he's like. He isn't like us. He's. . .'

'The proverbial rough diamond?' Emma asked, her mouth twisting. 'Oh grow up Camilla and don't be so silly, otherwise you'll end up like Mrs T.—a dyed-in-the wool snob. I'll go and see him for you, and I'll do what I can to calm him down. How do you intend to pay him back though? Could you manage monthly instalments from the allowance David is giving you?'

'I suppose so . . . I don't suppose you could persuade him to forget the money completely . . . I mean,' she wheedled, when Emma's mouth compressed, 'it isn't as though he needs it.'

'Maybe he doesn't *need* it, but you do *owe* it to him Camilla,' Emma told her bitingly, 'and in your shoes I should be only too anxious to pay it back and get it off my mind . . .'

'Oh you always were too "goody two shoes" to be true,' Camilla snapped crossly. 'David says you're a real school-marm type and that that's why you've opted for a career instead of marriage . . .'

'Oh does he?' Emma was thoroughly incensed, both by her sister's stupidity and by her smug assumption that once Emma had done her dirty work for her she could forget all about her responsibility for the accident.

'Well, let me tell you that I'd choose a career over marriage to David any day of the week . . . he's about as exciting as . . . as cold rice pudding . . .'

She regretted the words when Camilla got up and ran out of the kitchen, telling herself that she should not have taken her irritation out on her sister. Camilla was so absurdly sensitive to criticism, so much so that she occasionally wondered if the younger girl didn't use her 'sensitivity' as a weapon to get her own way. She glanced down at the solicitor's letter again, and frowned. She might as well get the ordeal over as quickly as possible. She picked it up and went through to her father's shabby study, quickly typing out a letter on his ancient machine, requesting an interview with Drake Harwood.

She had to go to London next week for her interview anyway, and with a bit of luck she might be able to combine the two appointments. She only hoped for Camilla's sake she was able to come to some arrangement with him. He couldn't be expected to forego the cost of the repairs altogether, and Camilla was selfish and blind to think he should, but if she could persuade him to accept payment by instalments ... if she could perhaps explain the reasons behind Camilla's rash behaviour. She sighed, remembering that her younger sister had bound her to silence. She would just have to play it by ear, she decided, sticking a stamp on the envelope and sealing it.

'Now remember, don't try any clever stuff, just be your natural self.'

Emma grimaced as she listened to her boss Robert Evans, giving her instructions concerning her forthcoming interview. 'And remember we'll all be rooting for you here. You've got more than a fair chance Emma... You're goodlooking, poised, intelligent, and you've got a personality of your own that comes across on the screen.'

Emma knew that everything he said was true, but even so she felt tensely anxious. She wanted to succeed at this interview, as much for Robert's sake as her own. He had been the one to give her first 'on screen' chance when she came to Television South. He had helped and encouraged her giving her the self-confidence to project herself well. He was forty-five and a burly, dark-haired man with a pleasant sense of humour and a keenly ambitious drive. Emma liked and admired him, and knew that if she had not been the person she was, or if her liking and respect had been less strong she could quite easily have been persuaded into an affair with him.

She admired him for his faithfulness to his wife—a quiet, serene woman she had met on several occasions. The temptations in a job like his must be never-ending and yet from somewhere he found the strength to resist them. Emma liked that in him. Her own strong moral code was due more to her own inner beliefs than being a vicar's daughter—their father had never tried to impose his faith on either her or Camilla; perhaps because she had had to grow up without a mother and be responsible for Camilla, Emma had formed her own moral code, based on her observations of life around her.

Her own self-respect was all important—without it she believed it was impossible for any human being to function properly. After all one had to live with oneself and her keenly honed ability to be self-critical was far sharper than any outside criticism she might have to face. An affair with a married man would be both messy and ultimately painful, but apart from that she could never feel completely comfortable in a relationship with someone else's husband, and then there was always the nagging doubt that having been unfaithful to her, how could he be expected to stay faithful to a mere mistress . . . No . . . such a role was not for her. She was acutely distrustful of sexual attraction; people so often mistook it for 'love' with disastrous results. She herself had never met a man she wanted so intensely that the need to make love with him over-rode everything else. Camilla thought her cold, even frigid, Emma knew differently but she respected her body sufficiently to listen to what it told her; and it told her it would never be happy with anything less than the best.

She had had menfriends; often dating people who worked for the television company, but always terminating the relationship when it threatened to get too intense. She had the reputation of an ambitious career woman, but it didn't worry her. Her career was important to her because it was a way of proving to herself her own ability but if she ever met a man who could fire both her emotions and her body; someone to whom she could give love and respect and who felt the same way about her, she suspected that all the energy she poured into her career would then go into her relationship with him. Sometimes the inner knowledge of her own intensity worried her; everyone thought she was so cool and controlled, but she didn't have chestnut hair for nothing. Her emotions were there all right, it was just that she had learned young the wisdom of leashing them under her own control.

She gave her boss a brilliant smile. 'I think everything's under control . . . right down to a new outfit for the big occasion.'

She had chosen her interview outfit with care. It was a beautifully cut fine wool suit in a sludgy nondescript olive that was a perfect foil for her hair and skin. The jacket was tailored and workmanlike, the skirt slim with a provocative slit at the front and back, just long enough to give a glimpse of her long legs—the suit combined both provocation and discretion, and it had amused her to buy it, knowing as she did that it was a contradiction of itself. If nothing else it should keep them guessing she thought drily, trying to concentrate on everything that Robert was telling her.

When she got home that night there was a letter
from Drake Harwood's solicitors waiting for her.
Mr Harwood was agreeable to seeing her, it told
her. An appointment had been made on the day
and at the time she had requested and that was a
relief.

When she told Camilla, her sister pouted sulkily
and complained that Emma was trying to make
her feel guilty. 'I'm trying to forget all about
that . . .' she told her, shuddering, 'and now you're
trying to make me remember.'

'I should have thought that was all too easy,'
Emma said drily, 'especially when it involved a bill
of several thousand pounds. Have you tried to talk
to David about it.'

'I can't. He'd understand, but his mother
wouldn't. Do you know what she said to me
today. . .?'

Emma closed her ears while Camilla set off on a
long diatribe against David's mother. The newly
married couple were to make their home at the
Manor with her. They were going to have their
own wing, and Camilla was already planning how
she would re-decorate and re-furnish it. If Mrs T.
allowed her to have anything other than very
traditional Colefax and Fowler plus assorted
antiques, she would be very surprised, Emma
thought, but kept her thoughts to herself. Camilla
thought that by marrying David she was gaining
the freedom to spend his money and buy herself all
the things she had never had, but what she was
really doing was entering a prison . . . However, it
was her own choice.

She had decided to spend the night before her
interview in London—that would save arriving

there with her clothes all creased from the train journey. She had booked herself a room at a fairly inexpensive hotel. Her father was busy writing his sermon when she went to tell him she was going. He looked up and smiled at her. The Reverend Richard Court had a vague, appealing smile. There had been several female parishioners eager to step into her mother's shoes, but he had managed to evade them all. Her father rather liked his bachelordom, Emma suspected. He had several friends at Oxford, dons with whom he spent long weekends re-living the days of their youth. He was also an avid reader. Outwardly gentle and mild, he possessed a core of inner steel. Emma suspected she had inherited from him. No one would ever persuade her father to do something he didn't wish to do. In many ways he was extremely selfish, but he was so gentle and mild, that very few people realised it. He was kind though and extremely adept at distancing himself from arguments and trouble. He could always see both sides of an argument—something else she had inherited from him Emma thought.

'I should be back tomorrow evening.' Her interview with the TV people was in the morning and she was seeing Drake Harwood after lunch.

'Camilla seems very anxious. I suppose it's all this fuss over the wedding.'

'She'll make a lovely bride. . .'

'Yes. Her one redeeming feature in Mrs T's eyes, no doubt,' he agreed, surprising Emma as he so often did by seeing what one had not believed that he had seen. 'It's lucky for her that she's so malleable. Marriage to a man like David would never do for you Emma.'

'No,' she agreed with a smile, 'I'm more likely to turn into another Mrs T.'

'I don't think so. No one could ever accuse you of being narrow-minded. I hope you get the job.'

Emma knew that he meant it, which was generous of him, because if she did she would have to find somewhere to live in London, and by removing herself from the vicarage she would deprive him of a housekeeper/secretary/general dogsbody. Being her father though, no doubt he would find someone else to take her place, with the minimum of fuss and inconvenience to himself.

She drove herself down to the station. It was only tiny and Joe the stationmaster promised to keep an eye on her car for her. 'Hope you get the job,' he told her, as he sold her her ticket. Everyone in the village probably knew why she was going to London—or at least thought they did. None of them knew of her appointment with Drake Harwood. It was ridiculous but she almost felt more apprehensive about that than she did about her interview for her new job.

The train arrived ten minutes late but was relatively empty. It took just over an hour and a half to reach London. Emma was both bored and stiff when it did. She allowed herself the extravagance of a taxi to her hotel, although she noticed that the driver looked less than impressed by its address. It seemed strange to think that if she got this job her face would be so familiar that almost everyone would recognise her. She wasn't sure yet how she would handle that sort of exposure. She liked her privacy and working for the local station had been able to preserve it. Robert had warned her against stressing too much how she felt about that. Perhaps it was something that one just grew accustomed to.

CHAPTER TWO

CONGRATULATING herself on her good timing Emma sat down gracefully in the chair indicated by the hovering secretary. Exactly three minutes to spare before the time appointed for her interview.

Across the other side of the room she caught sight of her own reflection in a mirrored section of wall surrounding an almost tropical plant display. The cool, graceful woman staring back at her was almost a stranger. She had never quite grown accustomed to the image she had learned to project during her years in the media, Emma reflected, hiding a rueful smile. As a teenager she had been gangly and awkward, lacking Camilla's blonde prettiness. It had been during her first job that an older colleague had suggested a grooming course at a local modelling school might be a good idea. At first she had been dismissive, but the advice had taken root and now she considered the money the course had cost her to be one of her best investments. She wasn't pretty and never would be, but knowing that she had learned to make the best of herself gave her a calm confidence which was reflected in the way she held her body and moved. What she never saw when she looked at herself was the purity of her bone structure and the sensual lure of the contrast between the dark russet of her hair, and her pale Celtic skin.

One or two curious glances came her way from

people passing through the foyer but Emma
ignored them. She knew she wasn't the only
candidate for the job, but they must have decided
to interview them all on separate days because she
was the only person waiting.

Having been kept waiting for the obligatory ten
minutes the discreet sound of a buzzer on the
secretary's desk heralded the commencement of
her ordeal.

The room she was shown into was large and
furnished in a modern high tech style. Three
people were already in the room. All of them men.
Robert had warned her against adopting a sexual
approach to the interview. 'I know you won't
anyway,' he had added, 'but just remember it's
brains they're looking for as well as looks.'

Emma hadn't needed the warning. She had
scorned using her sex to get her own way all her
life. In fact her father had once commented that
she was almost too direct. 'Men, on the whole,
enjoy having their egos massaged, my dear,' had
been his mild comment, one afternoon when she
had delivered a blisteringly disdainful look in the
direction of one of his parishioners. She had tried
to explain that she hadn't liked the way the man
had looked at her, or appreciated his heavy-
handed compliments, but her father had simply
shaken his head. 'Emma I suspect you're always
going to take the hard route through life.
Something in you demands that you meet
situations head on. Try to learn that sometimes it's
useful to have the ability to side-step them.' She
had now mastered the art, but it had been a hard-
won mastery, and she often had to bite her tongue
to stop herself from saying what she thought. 'Too

direct' other people had called her, while Camilla made no bones of her verdict. 'You're always so aggressive Emma,' she had told her once, 'and men don't like it.'

The interview progressed smoothly; she was able to answer all the questions put to her and she was also given the chance to air some of her own views, which she did cautiously. It was difficult to appear natural, when she knew that every movement, every inflection of her voice and manner was being studied to assess how appealing or otherwise it would appear to a viewer. Because that was what it all came down to—viewers, audience ratings . . . popularity.

She had promised herself before she left that she would be herself and that was what she tried to do. She was rewarded when her three interviewers stood up, signalling the end of her ordeal, and the most senior of them smiled broadly at her.

'I think you'll do us very nicely Emma,' he told her. 'I take it there won't be any problems with contracts or commitments to your present post?'

Her eyes widened fractionally. Was he offering her the job? What about the other applicants?

'None at all,' she managed to assure him crisply, 'but surely you'll want to . . .'

'You were our final interviewee, Emma,' another member of the trio interrupted. 'John here always believes in saving the best for last. In this case, I think he was right. If you have the time I'd like to take you down to our legal department so that we can run through a contract with you. There'll be a brief training period before you actually go on camera; we already know that you come across well. We'll have to take some publicity shots of you. There'll be a good deal of media interest of course. And a final word of warning ... unfair though this sounds, the public expect our women newsreaders to be, for the lack of a better description, morally sound, I think you know what I mean?'

Emma did. As Robert had told her she had nothing to fear on that score. 'You're not involved with a married man and you don't have any dubious lovers lurking in your past, so you should be okay there.'

She had remarked at the time on the unfairness of the double standard, but Robert had merely shaken his head and told her that that was the way things were.

'You'll come under a lot of pressure from the media, but anything you're dubious about, refer to us.'

She spent a further hour going over her contract; the salary she was being offered was reasonable rather than generous, but it should be enough to enable her to live in London, and there was a good wardrobe allowance.

'Initially at least, we'd like you to consult our wardrobe department about what you wear on screen.'

Nodding her head, Emma reflected wryly that even her taste had to be checked; nothing was going to be left to chance, but then the slot she was going to occupy on the new early evening programme was an important one, and it would be fighting for viewers against a long-established and very popular show on another channel.

'Now we'll leave you in peace,' she was told when they left the legal office. 'You'll need time to mull over everything that's happened. We won't need you here for another fortnight. Can you be ready to start then?'

They were in a corridor now and Emma automatically stepped to one side as a door opened and a man stepped through it. Tall and broad, he exuded an air of power and vitality. He nodded to the man accompanying Emma and then switched his attention to her, studying her with almost brutally open sexual appreciation. Strong though her control was, it wasn't strong enough to prevent the seep of angry colour into her skin. Her eyes fiercely grey in the frame of her face glared her resentment at him. The amused smile curling his mouth softened his features momentarily before his glance dropped to her breasts and lingered there quite blatantly.

Emma couldn't remember the last time she had felt so angry. She could feel the tension of it curling her fingers into talons, her tension increasing as she was forced to swallow her resentment down and force a coolly indifferent expression into her eyes as they met the knowing mockery in his. She had never seen anyone with such darkly green eyes before, she thought, hypnotised by them. Weren't green eyes a sign of a changeable, untrustworthy personality? The thought brought her a brief measure of satisfaction, quickly banished in the rage that almost choked her as he moved down the corridor and past her, deliberately allowing his body to brush against hers. There had been room for him to squeeze past without touching her, but he had not done so.

'I'm sorry we can't offer you lunch,' her companion was saying, 'but we have a busy

schedule this afternoon discussing a new series
we're thinking of buying.'

'That's all right,' Emma smiled automatically. 'I
have another appointment anyway.'

Outside the television building she debated
whether or not to go and ring Robert, and then
glancing at her watch decided not to. He would be
involved in preparations for the evening news
programme now, and besides her news would wait
until she got home. She wanted to savour it, to
relish the knowledge that she had succeeded, but
for some reason she could not.

It must be because she was so tensed up about
her interview with Drake Harwood, she decided,
looking round for a taxi. Once that was behind her
then she could relax and congratulate herself. As
she found one and waited for it to stop she
recalled the man in the corridor and her mouth
compressed.

Who on earth was he? Someone quite important.
She hadn't missed the vaguely subservient response
of her companion to his greeting. She frowned as
she stepped into her taxi. Why waste time thinking
about a man she was hardly likely to see again; he
wasn't the first man who had irritated her with his
attitude to her sex and he wouldn't be the last.

Not the first, but certainly the most blatant. Her
skin tingled with renewed impotent rage as she
recalled the mockery in his jade eyes. He had
known exactly how furious she was and he had
enjoyed her fury. She couldn't remember the last
time she had seen such an aggressively sexual
male. Not her type at all, she thought disdainfully,
giving the driver the address of the modest
restaurant where she had decided to have lunch.

She was quite content to lunch alone. She had a lot to think about and a lot to plan. She would have to find somewhere to live; sharing at first perhaps, and then later, she could find her own place. She did some quick sums on the back of an old envelope. She would need new clothes, but hopefully not too many. She had quite a good wardrobe, preferring to buy classic rather than fashion clothes and suspected that these would be in keeping with the image she would be expected to project. Her full mouth compressed slightly as she remembered what she had been told. Why was it perfectly acceptable for a man to possess a murky past but not for a woman? Luckily there was nothing at all in her past or present that could be used by the press. Her thoughts flashed to the man in the corridor. Undoubtedly the same could not be said for him. Her mouth curved in a cynical smile. Stop thinking about him, she chided herself eating the seafood salad she had ordered.

She took her time over her lunch, forcing down the jittery nerves clamouring in her stomach. She was more tense over this coming interview than she had been over this morning's. Damn Camilla, she thought exasperatedly, not for the first time. What on earth had possessed her to take the man's car in the first place, never mind crashing it?

She grimaced faintly to herself. She could just imagine her younger sister's reaction on wakening to find herself in a strange bed. Mrs T. held very strong views on what she considered to be the lack of morals among the younger generation. In time David would be very like his mother; humourless and rigorously strait-laced. Cynically she wondered if Camilla was telling her the entire truth. Her sister had had a positive phalanx of boyfriends before she became engaged to David. She enjoyed flirting with and teasing the male sex and was nowhere near as innocent as her blonde delicacy implied. She had admitted that Drake Harwood had shown an interest in her. On the other hand it could be perfectly feasible that she had simply had too much to drink and that he had dumped her in a spare bedroom to sleep it off. It all depended. Whatever the case he certainly didn't appear to be inclined to treat Camilla with indulgence now. His solicitor's letter had been starkly uncompromising. Finishing her coffee and settling her bill Emma stood up, and glanced at her watch. She had half an hour before her appointment with him . . . it was time to go.

The block of offices her taxi driver took her to was everything one would expect for a going-places entrepreneur. Brashly new, the impressive foyer was designed to intimidate and impress. The receptionist looked as though she had just stepped out of *Vogue*, and eyed Emma unresponsively as she walked towards her.

At the sound of Drake Harwood's name she perked up a little. No doubt *she* was a far cry from the women normally asking to see him Emma reflected dourly. He had been mentioned in the gossip columns quite a lot recently, and she had read that he was currently escorting one of the 'models' featured in his newly acquired magazine. Although she had no deep-rooted objection to members of her sex making a living from capitalising on whatever they considered their most saleable assets to be, she viewed the men who made their living selling the female form both in the flesh and on celluloid with considerable distaste. It was true that Drake Harwood had merely gained control of his girlie magazine as part of a larger package, but he had been quick to accept the challenge thrown down by the rival magazine and to boast that he would soon boost its ailing circulation.

Emma didn't doubt that most of the women who posed for such magazines did so with their eyes open—witness Fiona's determined attempts to catch Drake Harwood's attention—but for herself ... Only last summer Camilla had commented on what she called her 'prudishness' when she had refused to go topless during their holiday in France. 'Everyone does ...' had been her younger sister's critical comment. Maybe, but Emma had never been one to follow the general herd. Her own body was something she rarely thought about. Camilla had laughed when she insisted on wearing a swimsuit, but her skin was fair and burned easily.

'Mr Harwood will see you now. Go up in the far lift,' the receptionist directed in bored accents. Reminding herself that she was twenty-six years old and had just been offered the sort of job which ought to boost anyone's self-confidence, Emma stepped into the lift and pressed the single button, hoping that the fluttering in her stomach was as a result of the upward surge of the lift rather than her own nervousness.

A secretary as elegant as the girl in the foyer was waiting for her; blonde hair immaculately in place.

'This way please.' She knocked briefly on a door and then held it open.

The room Emma walked into was enormous,

with a panoramic view over the rooftops of
London. The decor was almost austere; the
rosewood desk huge; the Beber carpet underfoot a
masculine blend of russets and browns.

'Miss Court. . .' He took advantage of her
momentary consternation to ask mockingly, 'I
take it you did get the job? I shall look forward to
seeing you on screen when the new programme
goes out.'

She had recognised him instantly of course, but
it had taken her several seconds to assimilate the
fact that the man in the corridor of the television
building and Drake Harwood were one and the
same. Remembering his open sexual inspection of
her, she felt her face burning with a mixture of
tension and anger. He had obviously known *then*
who she was. Tension sharpened her instincts.
How had he known about the job though? She
recalled the muted deference in her companion's
manner towards him and anxiety feathered along
her nerves. If he wanted her to comment on the
coincidence; on the fact that he knew about her
new job, he was going to be disappointed.
Exciting Fiona had called him, according to
Camilla, and she could understand why. If ever a
man exuded sexuality it was this one, she thought
clinically. His hair was thick and dark, almost
unruly as it grew low into his nape. Even seated he
gave the impression of height and breadth. His suit
was expensively tailored, discreetly dark and
Saville Row, and yet it left an unmistakable
impression of solid muscle and bone; a legacy from
his early days working on building sites, she
decided. His skin was olive toned and tanned, the
bones shaping his face arrogantly masculine. Even

without those green eyes she would have been
wary of him. He was a man whose every
movement revealed a raw pleasure in his masculinity; a man who would never consider a
woman to be his equal, Emma thought drily.

'Like what you see?' His words left her in no
doubt that he was aware of her scrutiny. Emma
fought down the urge to snap back that she
disliked everything about him, and said instead,
'It's always interesting to come face to face with
the people one reads about in the press.'

'Really?' His eyebrows rose. 'Surely you aren't
admitting that you succumb to hero-worship Miss
Court. Somehow I can't see you in that role.'

She wasn't admitting anything of the sort and
he knew it damn him. Angrily Emma suppressed
an inclination to bite out that far from hero-
worshipping, she was more likely to find herself
criticising him, and reminded herself of the
purpose of her appointment.

'Quite a coincidence, our meeting twice in the
one day.'

Emma had the distinct feel that he was toying
with her in some way, playing a game which was
giving him huge amusement and not a little
masculine satisfaction.

'They do happen.' She was fighting to control
her responses. Instinct told her she would need all
her wits about her to match this man. 'As you
know from my letter, I wanted to discuss my sister
with you. You may remember, she had a slight
accident in your car.'

She had wanted to get him off the subject of *her*
and on to the subject of Camilla and she had
succeeded. His eyes sharpened, his eyebrows lifting

tauntingly. 'A *slight* accident? Is that how you describe theft and several thousand pounds worth of damage? Why hasn't she come to see me herself?'

Not for the first time it crossed Emma's mind that the whole thing might simply be a ploy to get to know Camilla better—on his own terms, with him calling the tune. He would demand that sort of relationship she guessed intuitively; he would derive satisfaction from knowing that he was the one in command. Well he might as well know from the start where he stood with Camilla.

'She asked me to come because she doesn't want her fiancé to know anything about what happened.'

If he was disappointed to learn that Camilla was engaged, he wasn't showing it.

'And what did happen?' he asked softly. 'I have wondered . . . The first I knew of anything was when the police rang me to say that my car had been involved in an accident. Quite a surprise, as you can imagine.'

'Camilla attended one of your parties. It seems that she had rather too much to drink.' She managed to say it quite calmly, but could not bring herself to look at him. 'When she woke up in the morning and found herself in a strange bed, she panicked a little I'm afraid . . .'

'She did? I wonder why,' he mused sardonically. 'I take it this strange bed contained no one other than herself?'

'Not as far as I know.' Let him make what he liked of that.

'And this er . . . panic . . . motivated her into stealing my car.'

Stealing wasn't the word Emma would have used, but she forced herself not to say so. 'It was very early in the morning. She didn't want to draw attention to herself by calling a taxi . . . I'm afraid she was in too much of a panic to think things through properly.'

'Unlike her sister, who I'm sure never does anything without doing so.' The way he said it, it wasn't a compliment. 'I take it this panic was on account of her fiancé. She doesn't want him to know she spent the night at my house is that it? Seems an odd relationship to have with a prospective husband. Why is she marrying him?'

'Because she loves him.'

His eyebrows really did rise then. 'My, my, does she so . . . But not obviously to the extent of being able to tell him the truth.'

'There are complications.' Emma knew she sounded brusque. 'They need not concern you. Camilla wanted me to ask you if you would be prepared to take instalment payments to cover the repairs to your car. She can't afford to repay you in a lump sum. She simply doesn't have that sort of money.'

'But her fiancé does, presumably, otherwise she wouldn't be marrying him.'

The cynicism in his voice prompted Emma to snap, 'Yes he does, but naturally she wouldn't want to ask him to lend her such a sum before they are married, if that's what you were going to suggest. The repayments will include an interest element, if that's what's worrying you.'

'No, it does not worry me Miss Court, since I'm not prepared to accept them.' He got up and came towards her, surprisingly deft in his movements for such a tall man. 'However, if your sister genuinely can't repay me in cash, I am prepared to take another form of payment . . .'

He was watching her closely, and Emma burst out rashly, 'If you think Camilla will agree to have sex with you in return for you dropping the charges, you're way, way off course . . .'

'And so are you,' he told her smoothly, 'the payment I was thinking of wasn't so much your sister's body in my bed, as yours . . . in my magazine.'

For a moment Emma genuinely thought she might faint. She looked at him, grey eyes dazed and disbelieving, hot colour running up under her skin as she realised he was perfectly serious.

'Me? But . . . but I'm not a model, I don't . . .' She shook her head trying to sort out her muddled thoughts.

'Don't what,' he mocked her, 'take your clothes off for financial gain? But of course you don't Miss Court, that's what will make the fact that you're featuring in the magazine such a sales booster. I've been looking for something to up our ratings, and you could be just the thing.'

He was prowling round her now, studying her, stripping the clothes from her body with a careless masculine arrogance that made her long to smack him.

'Yes, I can see the captions now. Cool newsreader Emma Court, as you've never seen her before . . . except perhaps in dreams. It should make an extremely good feature.'

'You must be mad!'

He laughed mirthlessly, 'How predictable of you, somehow I had expected better. No, I'm far from mad Emma Court.'

'You knew who I was this morning, didn't you?' she demanded furiously, remembering the way he had looked at her then, probably already anticipating this very moment.

He was coolly amused. 'My dear girl, I knew everything there was to know about you ten minutes after I'd read your letter.'

Emma thought furiously. 'Did you arrange for me to get that job. . .? Did you?'

He smiled infuriatingly, 'How quick you are Emma, I like that in a woman, it saves so much tedious time wasting. What does it matter? You've got it haven't you?'

'And now you plan to use me to . . .'

'I'm offering you what you came here for,' he told her curtly, 'if the terms of payment are unacceptable to you, you can always refuse . . .'

'And if I do, you'll sue Camilla?'

He shrugged. 'Do I look like a man who'd let someone rob me of several thousand pounds and do nothing about it? Half the secret of being successful Emma Court is comprised of luck—pure and simple. I consider myself to be more lucky than most. The very day your letter arrived, I was trying to think of ways to boost the magazine's circulation, bringing it a little more upmarket. I don't know if you are aware of it, but a rival of mine has challenged me to beat his circulation figures.'

'Yes, I am aware of it.' Her response was terse. 'But I can't see how nude photographs of me . . .'

'Of you, Emma Court, no,' he agreed, interrupting swiftly, 'but of you Emma Court, the new anchorwoman of *"Newsview"*, yes. On screen you project a very cool, remote image, Emma. I know,

I've made it my business to watch you. A lot of men find that very ... challenging. The fact that we are able to show them a different Emma ...'

'No!' The denial burst past her lips before she could stop it, her eyes wide and haunted as she faced him. 'I'd never agree to anything like that,' she told him fiercely.

'No?' He picked up his telephone receiver. 'Very well then, I'll instruct my solicitors to continue with the charges against your sister and to ensure that they get as much media coverage as possible ...'

She knew he wasn't bluffing. He had the power to do exactly what he was threatening. She could just imagine Mrs T's face when she read what Camilla had done, and no doubt the press would have a field day making it sound even worse than it was. She was sorely tempted to go home and tell Camilla that she had been unsuccessful, but the thought of her sister's hysterics; the knowledge that it could well mean the end of her engagement—because Mrs T. would put unholy pressure on David to break the engagement, she knew—overwhelmed her.

Forcing herself to think calmly and quickly, and to detach herself from what was happening she viewed her options, and could only come up with one solution. Damn Drake Harwood and damn Camilla. She would have to agree, she decided bitterly. She had no real choice. Let him take his photographs, but he'd never be able to use them in the way he'd planned.

Bitter anger tensed her muscles as she envisaged having to explain to Robert why she could not take the job ... but he would understand. They wouldn't want her on local television either . . . not once Drake Harwood had splashed her photograph all over his magazine. So what, she told herself hardily, she would be able to find another job in some other field where her public image wasn't so important and at least she would have the satisfaction of defeating Drake Harwood. As he had said himself, photographs of her, as herself would have little appeal. As Emma Court she was no one and even though her mind and body screamed objections to what she would have to do she must ignore them.

'Well?'

She faced him coolly, 'I agree. but first I must have a document signed by you, clearing Camilla from any charges you might make against her.'

'You shall have it. I do admire a woman of keen perception Emma Court. Somehow I thought you and I would be able to reach a mutually acceptable agreement.'

He was taunting her, Emma was sure of it, but she wasn't going to respond.

'How long will it take to get the document prepared and signed,' she asked him coolly. She must know how much time she had. She daredn't say that she wasn't taking the job until she had that paper in her hand.

He was watching her face. 'It will be given to you immediately after the photographic session.'

'Do I have your word on that?' Her eyes were hard, and she noted the dull flush colouring his cheek bones.

'You have it,' he told her crisply. 'Now let's get down to the arrangements shall we?'

* * *

He obviously didn't believe in wasting any time Emma thought hollowly half an hour later as she left his office. Tomorrow she had to present herself at a studio whose address he had given her, and he had promised that she would also receive the documents releasing Camilla while she was there.

She went back to her hotel and booked in for another night. Then she telephoned home and told her father she had been delayed. 'Camilla wants to speak to you,' he told her.

Camilla sounded tense. 'Did you see him?' she demanded.

'Yes, and he's agreed to drop all the charges.' There wasn't much point in telling her sister the price she was having to pay for her freedom. There was nothing martyred or self-sacrificing in her decision; it was simply the only one she could make. She had grown so used to protecting Camilla that it was almost second nature.

She put off telephoning Robert, her interview with him was best left until she got home. Thank goodness she hadn't actually signed a new contract. The television company would be more than pleased to let her go when they knew why she was leaving. Once her photograph had appeared in Drake Harwood's obnoxious publication no serious television station would want to touch her with a bargepole. Bitterness welled up inside her, but she fought it down; at least she would have the satisfaction of defeating his main purpose and that, she sensed, was something very few people ever did. He had been quite cold and callous about his reasons for what he was doing; *her* thoughts and feelings meant nothing to him and neither did the fact that he was destroying her career. She had sensed beneath the mockery a fine contempt of the female sex, and she shuddered inwardly, trying not to think about the ordeal to come.

That evening after she had had her bath she forced herself to study her nude reflection in the bedroom mirror. Her body was slender and well formed, unmistakably feminine; the thought of exposing it to the eyes of some jaded photographer made her shudder with distaste. If only she could blot the whole thing out of her mind somehow . . . but that wasn't possible.

Neither was sleep; she lay awake for what felt like hours, prey to her thoughts and too-active imagination. It was difficult to visualise anything more degrading than what she was going to have to do, and her pride rebelled fiercely against it, but there was no escape.

CHAPTER THREE

MORNING came; she was heavy eyed and lethargic. The thought of breakfast held no appeal and having showered she dressed quickly in plain cream underwear. The moment her fingers touched the pale, silky fabric she started to shiver. Dear God, she could not go through with this; she could not subject herself to such sexual debasement. She ran to the bathroom and retched painfully, shuddering convulsively afterwards. If only she could simply walk out of this hotel and away from ... from everything, she thought tiredly, but she couldn't. She had spent too many years as Camilla's older sister to do that. She could not desert the younger girl now.

A blessed numb calm seemed to engulf her the moment she walked outside; it was like being encased in a soft plastic bubble; safe from all harm; from all contact with her own feelings.

The taxi drive to the address Drake Harwood had given her was over all too soon. The studio was housed in an elegant Regency terrace; testament to how much money could be made from their business, Emma reflected bitterly as she paid off the taxi driver and rang the bell.

It took several minutes for the door to open. A girl of about her own age stood there, dressed in tatty jeans and a bulky sweater. 'Hi, come on in,' she directed. 'Drake warned me to expect you.' She gave Emma a wide grin. 'Feeling nervous?

42

Drake said you might be. This way.'

Following her down a narrow corridor, Emma gritted her teeth against the biting retort she was longing to make. Her relief at discovering that the photographer was another woman had quickly been displaced by fury that Drake Harwood should discuss her with her.

'In here . . .'

'Here . . .' was an expensively equipped studio, dominated by the large bed on which several spotlights were focused. The bed itself was covered in a satin spread, the colour of rich cream.

'Drake's idea. I'm Pat Devlin,' the other girl introduced herself. 'I don't normally accept commissions of this type, but Drake made me an offer I couldn't refuse, as the saying goes. That was his idea,' she added gesturing towards the bed and grimacing faintly. 'He said the spread would be a perfect foil for your hair. Fancy a cup of coffee?'

Nodding numbly, Emma tried to come to grips with reality. It seemed impossible to believe this was actually happening but it was . . . and there was no escape.

'Oh and Drake left something for you, said I was to give it to you after we'd finished. It's over there.'

Emma looked at the thick envelope. So he had kept his promise to her. Somehow she had never doubted that he would. 'Hey are you feeling okay?' There was genuine anxiety in the question.

Emma nodded her head. 'First time nerves,' she grimaced.

'And second thoughts. Why not have third ones and forget the whole thing. It's none of my

business of course, but if you're really hating the
thought of it as much as you look as though you
are, it will show in the photographs, and no matter
how much Drake is paying you, it can't possibly
compensate for what it's costing you . . .'

'I have to do it.'

Emma knew her voice was shaking. She couldn't
look at Pat, just in case she broke down and gave
in to her suggestion not to go through with it. The
papers were there and she could take them, but
pride would not let her. She had to go through
with it . . . but if Drake Harwood chose to print
the finished product it would not be of Emma
Court, TV newsreader, but simply Emma Court,
out of work. He had demanded a price and she
was prepared to pay it, but she wasn't prepared to
involve anyone else in that payment.

'Okay, then let's get it over with shall we?'

Pat Devlin might not be used to doing the sort
of work Drake had engaged her for, but she was a
professional to her finger-tips Emma realised in
the two hours that followed. Small, and wiry with
a shock of thick black hair, she possessed an
energy that left Emma limp.

'Take your hair down,' she had instructed,
helping Emma to uncoil her chignon, after she had
taken some initial shots of Emma as she had
arrived at the studio.

'Look,' she asked in a kind voice when she had
asked her to undress, 'are you sure . . .'

'Sure.'

'Okay then.'

If it wasn't as bad as she had dreaded it was bad
enough. Drake's magazine was apparently more
up-market than many of its competitors and for

that reason she had been instructed to make sure all the shots were in good taste, Pat told Emma with a grimace. 'Personally if I had my way the things would be banned, but a girl has to make a living. He was right about your hair,' she added when she had positioned Emma on the satin spread. 'I think you'd better close your eyes,' she added, 'they give away too much. You're supposed to look as though you're enjoying this, not on the rack. Try to think of something pleasant . . .'

All she could think of was that at some future date, Drake Harwood would be looking at her like this. The thought made her so tense that Pat had to stop work. What was one man among thousands, Emma jeered at herself, glad of the mug of coffee Pat brought her.

'Nearly over,' she encouraged her. 'God I remember the first nude shots I ever did . . . I was nearly sick with nerves . . . but after a while you get used to it . . .'

Emma shuddered again, thankful when at last her ordeal was over and she could discard the cream satin underwear Pat had asked her to wear. The satin was soft and of excellent quality, the underwear perfectly respectable, sexy, but in an understated way; the sort of thing she herself might even have worn, for a lover perhaps . . . but now the mere thought of it against her body revolted her. All she wanted to do was to immerse herself in a tub of hot water and scrub her skin until she felt clean again.

Unfortunately, it would not be as easy to erase the morning from her mind.

'Okay, here's your envelope, don't forget it,' Pat instructed handing it to her when Emma emerged from behind the changing screen.

'I'll just pack up my things and then I'll be on my way too. You know you meet all types in this game, but you ... you're someone I just can't pigeonhole. You went through agony there, and yet you kept on ... why?'

When Emma shook her head, Pat shrugged. 'Well I guess it's your own affair. I'd better get back to my flat and get these developed before Drake starts screaming for them. It's the first time I've done this sort of work for him. Industrial stuff's more his line. Still it makes a change from working for *Vogue*, and photographing building sites.'

'Well come on, I want to hear all about it.'

The first thing Emma had done when she got home was to ring Robert. Now they were sitting in the bar of a quiet local pub, nursing their drinks.

'I can't take the job.' She hadn't meant to say it so baldly, but somehow the words were out and Robert was staring at her as though she had lost her mind.

'Emma have you gone mad. Of course you can take it... They offered it to you, I know that, and it's the chance of a life-time, just what you've always wanted.'

'Just what I did always want,' Emma corrected unsteadily, 'I've ... I've changed my mind ...'

Robert glared at her as though he was seeing her for the first time. 'I see, and is one allowed to ask why? Don't tell me,' he continued furiously, 'it has to be a man. God Emma, I thought you were different, I thought you had more sense, but it seems I was wrong. I thought you wanted a career, not ...'

'Love?' she supplemented drily. 'All women want that, Robert . . .'

Although Robert had leapt to the wrong conclusion, it was easier to let him go on believing it than to try and find some alternative explanation for her decision. Inside she felt sick and shaky, one part of her longing to pour out to him her pain and misery, and another warning her against doing so; against crossing the careful barrier she had always maintained between them.

Emma wasn't blind; she was aware that Robert was attracted to her, it would be easy to push that attraction into something more because she needed someone to confide in and comfort her, but if she did they would both end up regretting it. Robert loved his wife, and she wanted no part of a man who was committed to someone else.

'Well I hope to God he knows what you're giving up,' Robert said harshly, draining his glass. 'What do you intend to do now? Stay on with us?'

Emma shook her head. 'No that's not possible I'm afraid . . .'

'Lover-boy wants a little stay at home wife, is that it?' Robert practically snarled the words. 'Very well Emma, if that's what you want . . .'

'I'll give you my notice tomorrow.' She had to bend her head to hide from him the tears starting up in her eyes.

'If that's what you want. . . .'

It isn't what I want, her heart cried out rebelliously, but it's what I have to do . . . I don't have any alternative. If she kept quiet and signed her new contract, they would have to abide by it; they would not be able to get rid of her, as they would want to do, once the magazine came out,

and she had too much pride to subject herself or
them to that.

Robert drove her home in a stiff silence. She
had holidays owing to her which meant that she
need not work her notice period. When she told
her father and Camilla, neither seemed overly
concerned.

'Oh good, you'll be able to help with the
wedding arrangements,' was Camilla's selfish
remark, while her father commented that it would
be nice to have her at home.

'I still can't believe that tomorrow David and I will
be married,' Camilla said for the umpteenth time.
They were in her bedroom, Emma doing her
packing for the Caribbean honeymoon David was
taking her on. 'Thank God you were able to
persuade that beast Drake Harwood to drop
charges.'

It was the first time Camilla had referred to
Drake Harwood in the month since Emma's
return from London.

'It's a shame that you wouldn't be my
bridesmaid, David says his best man is an old
friend from school—he comes from a frightfully
wealthy family.'

'Mrs T. wanted you to have young attendants,
and I think she was right, David's twin cousins
will look adorable.'

'I just hope that the weather keeps fine,' Camilla
continued fretfully.

The reception was being held in a marquee in
the Manor grounds, and several fine June days
had dried out the lawns and warmed up the air.
The Manor would make a perfect setting for the

occasion Emma admitted; Mrs T. was over the moon because she had persuaded Lady Cornwald and her husband to attend. In fact, apart from herself everyone seemed perfectly happy.

Since her return from London she had heard nothing from Drake Harwood. She had held her breath for a couple of days after the announcement of the new newsgirl had been made, half expecting to suffer the effects of his pique, but when a week went past and she had heard nothing, her jangling nerves settled down again. Doubtless he realised that there was simply nothing he could do. A rather unusual feeling for him, she reflected with acid satisfaction. It would do him good to be on the receiving end of what he was so fond of giving to others.

That he could have made her ordeal worse for her, she was forced to admit; there had been nothing personal in his humiliation of her, Emma knew that . . . No, that quick entrepreneurial brain of his had simply seen her as another asset; another commodity he could capitalise on.

Press interest in the previously much vaunted contest between *Macho* and its rival had died, confirming Emma's opinion that at least a good seventy-five per cent of it had been carefully organised publicity.

Once Camilla was safely married, she would have to start looking round for another job. One of her father's university lecturer friends was looking for a research assistant to help him with a project he had taken on for the summer recess, and Emma was toying with the idea of offering her services. She had a good degree in political science and the project promised to be quite interesting.

She couldn't stay at home playing surrogate vicar's wife for ever, she acknowledged, admitting ruefully to herself that her father, with all his charming lazy selfishness, was already inclined to expect her to take on many of his duties. At the moment she was enjoying them, but she knew that eventually they would pall.

Her secretarial skills were good, although perhaps slightly dulled. She wasn't too sure how good her shorthand speed would be after several years' neglect for instance, but it had occurred to her that perhaps a secretarial job at Westminster might be appealing—always supposing she could get one—and might serve as a jumping block to other things.

Only one thing was sure, and that was that she could not go back into television. If she did, every job she managed to land in front of the camera would raise the spectre of Drake Harwood's photographs being re-published. Something like that was just the sort of material the gutter-press loved to get their hands on. No ... if she could find herself some congenial work for long enough for the publicity to die down, she could then start to re-think her future career. Of course she was bitterly disappointed about what had happened and about losing Robert's friendship; he had had every right to be angry with her after he had promoted her career so intensely, and she could have explained to him, but pride would not let her. Perhaps in her secret heart she had hoped that he might object; that he might dig deep enough for the truth to have to come out, but he had accepted her explanation at face value, and in many ways that hurt.

The day of the wedding dawned fine and clear; a perfect June morning complete with cuckoo calls, Emma reflected drowsily, hearing the bird song through her open bedroom window. Fortune had a way of shining benevolently on her younger sister, although Camilla was the last person to think so.

Getting up and donning jeans and a T-shirt Emma hurried downstairs. Camilla had requested the traditional bridal breakfast in bed—the fact that Emma was supposed to go up to the house and give Mrs T. a hand with the caterers had somehow seemed to escape the younger woman's memory.

Sighing Emma opened the kitchen door to let Puss in Boots, the cat, out. The sunshine was still faintly hazy, promising the heat to come. On a morning like this there was nowhere to beat the English countryside, she reflected, enjoying the solitude and breathing in the clean air. Although she loved the frantic bustle and pace of city life, there was no doubt that it was good to get back to nature at times, to slow one's pace down and live in harmony with one's surroundings.

Her father was awake when she went upstairs with his breakfast. He was to conduct the service in the small local church and a very distant second cousin of the family had been coerced into giving Camilla away in his stead. That this distant relative was from the upper echelons of the family tree had greatly pleased Mrs T., although Emma wondered wryly if she would be quite as pleased when she discovered how eccentric Uncle Ted could be. To the best of her knowledge she had never seen him wearing anything other than a particularly hairy and ancient looking brown tweed suit which looked as though he had inherited it from one of his ancestors.

Morning suits for the men was the order of the day; Uncle Ted had been apprised of this, but just to be on the safe side, Emma had taken the precaution of hiring one for him, and was hoping that she had managed to gauge his size correctly.

Camilla was still asleep when she went in, her peaches and cream skin glowing, her blonde hair curling wildly over the pillow. She woke up when Emma called her. David was at least getting value for money as far as physical attractiveness went, Emma reflected, as Camilla slid out of bed.

Dainty and femininely curved, Camilla took great care to ensure that her figure remained perfect. Watching her pout anxiously as she studied a non-existent spot Emma prayed that the marriage would be successful and that Camilla would not grow bored and spoilt. David would pet and indulge her, which was what she wanted, and if she had the good sense to appreciate him for what he was her life should be a very happy one.

She doubted that Camilla loved David in the way that she would want to love any man with whom she shared her life, but then for all her prettiness and sex appeal, Emma had always considered that Camilla lacked her own intensity and depth of emotional need. Perhaps it was just as well, she reflected. The shallows of life were always much safer than the depths.

'Be an angel and lay my underwear out for me will you,' Camilla called on her way to the bathroom. 'The hairdresser's due at ten, and he's bringing a girl with him to do my make-up . . . so I'd better have my shower now.'

The underwear was new and delicately white. She and Camilla had bought it from an expensive shop just off Bond Street. It had been Emma's trousseau present to her sister, but now, extracting it from its tissue wrappings, Emma could not repress a shudder of distaste, remembering the cream satin that had clung so lovingly to her skin.

'I've got to go up to the house and help Mrs T.,' she called as she passed the bathroom. 'I'll be back just as soon as I can . . .'

'Emma don't stay there too long . . . Uncle Ted should be arriving soon and you know he bores me to tears . . . and then there's the flowers and. . .'

Closing her ears to Camilla's petulant voice Emma let herself out of the house. It was only a ten minute drive to the Manor and at this time of the morning she had the road to herself apart from the milkman who called out a cheery greeting to her. 'Nice day for the wedding,' he commented. 'I've just been up at the Manor. Chaos it is . . .'

Emma could well believe it. Despite her love of organising Mrs T. had a knack of turning order into chaos. The middle-aged cousin whom she employed as companion/social secretary was the person on whom the burden for most of the arrangements had fallen. Emma liked Laura Petts. Although quiet and self-effacing she was an intelligent, and, on occasions, witty person. How on earth she endured Mrs T.'s domineering manner, Emma had no idea.

It was Laura who greeted her when she walked into the Manor, giving her a quiet smile.

'All under control?' Emma asked.

'More or less. They put the marquee up last night and the caterers arrived on time. They've practically taken over the kitchen, and it looks as though the weather is going to be kind to us. How's Camilla?'

'Looking very bridal,' Emma told her. 'What can I do to help?'

'You might go downstairs for me and check on how Mrs Berry's getting on with breakfast. We've got nearly a dozen people staying here and what with the caterers and all the unaccustomed activity . . .'

'I'll go down now.'

Mrs Berry looked flustered and cross when Emma walked into the kitchen. 'Having all these folks to stay . . . as if I hadn't got enough to do . . .'

Having managed to soothe her down, Emma went back upstairs. The two small girls who were to be Camilla's attendants were up and dressed. Both pretty blondes they would look delightful in the spotted voile dresses Camilla had chosen for them. Her own dress was a lavish *Gone with the Wind* confection trimmed with antique lace and matching ribbons. It had cost a fortune, but she looked like a dream in it.

Having ascertained that there was nothing more she could do, and feeling that she had fulfilled any obligation she might have towards Mrs T., Emma was just on the point of leaving when the latter came hurrying downstairs. Tall and well built, there were times when she reminded Emma of a battleship under full steam.

'Emma . . . you weren't going were you?'

'Everything seems to be under admirable control,' Emma responded with a smile. 'Laura is doing a sterling job isn't she? I thought I'd better get back to check on Uncle Ted and father. You know what men can be like.'

'Yes . . . yes of course . . .' She frowned. 'I really had hoped you could stay to check on the flowers for me . . . I told the florists exactly what was needed, but one can never rely entirely on these people.'

'I'm sure everything will be fine,' Emma soothed.

'I do hope so. My poor head is aching already. There is just so much to do . . . Oh by the way my dear, your friend telephoned, and asked if it was all right if he came. . . I must say I was a little surprised, but of course, I agreed. He sounds quite charming . . .'

Her friend? Who on earth was she talking about Emma wondered curiously. The only person she could think of was Robert. Her heart lifted. Had he perhaps had second thoughts; realised that there must be more to her leaving than he had first thought. It cheered her considerably that he had wanted to see her enough to ring Mrs T. and invite himself to the wedding. It was a curiously unRobert-like manoeuvre, and even though she knew it would be impossible for her to change her mind, she was still glad that he had apparently seen through her deception.

The service was being conducted at one o'clock and by twelve Emma was beginning to wonder if she was ever going to be ready on time. The yellow silk suit she was wearing was hanging upstairs in her room, but she was still no nearer getting into it

than she had been at ten. Uncle Ted, as she had
suspected, had arrived in his brown suit, and it
had taken a considerable degree of cajoling to get
him into the morning suit she had hired. Once in
it, he presented a surprisingly dapper figure, his
silver hair gleaming.

A step on the stairs warned her that the
hairdresser and his assistant were on the point of
departing. A large bouquet of red roses had
arrived from David and Emma took them up to
her sister, finding her sitting in front of her mirror
pouting dangerously.

'My hair looks awful,' she cried out when
Emma walked in. 'And just look at the mess that
frightful girl's made of my make-up.'

'You look stunning,' Emma told her, studying
her immaculate hairstyle and make-up, 'and look
David's sent you these . . .'

The red roses got little more than a cursory
glare. 'What about Uncle Ted, did you
manage . . .'

'He looks every inch the elegant gentleman,'
Emma assured her. 'How would you like a glass of
champagne?'

Without waiting for Camilla's response she went
downstairs to open the bottle she had bought
purposely for the occasion. Knowing Camilla as
she did, she had decided that a couple of glasses
would do wonders to relax her highly-strung
nerves, and although Camilla pulled a face, by the
time she was ready to get into her dress, she was
considerably more at ease.

Emma was now dressed herself. Her yellow silk
suit with its straight skirt and blouson jacket was a
perfect foil for her chestnut hair, which unlike

Camilla's had had to be content with its normal shampoo and blow dry. But then who was going to be looking at her? Emma mocked herself.

Camilla looked like a fairy princess in her dress, there was no doubt about that.

It was a view that was reinforced by the soft sounds of appreciation filling the church when Camilla walked down the aisle on her cousin's arm. Emma was sitting at the front, taking the place that would have been their mother's. Because she had had to be at the church early she had not been able to spot Robert—for all she knew he might only be intending to attend the reception. What was she getting so excited about she chided herself; nothing could change her decision. When, she wondered, would Drake Harwood publish her photographs? She shuddered deeply, suddenly cold.

At last the service was over and everyone was getting into cars for the journey to the Manor. Emma was driving her father and Uncle Ted. As she drove out into the road her eye was caught by a wickedly scarlet Ferrari parked just outside the church, and her heart thudded.

Oh stop being ridiculous, she chided herself. Of course it wouldn't be Drake Harwood's . . . what on earth would *he* be doing at Camilla's wedding? They barely knew one another. No it probably belonged to one of David's jet-setting ex-school friends.

They were among the first to arrive and having assured herself that Uncle Ted would be on hand to participate in the formal receiving line Emma wandered into the house, glancing appreciatively at the wedding presents which were set out in the

drawing room. It was cool and quiet inside away
from the mêlée of guests arriving but she could not
stay here for ever.

Sighing Emma went back outside, dazzled
momentarily by the strong sunlight.

'Emma my dear, where have you been
hiding. . .?'

There was no escape from Mrs T. Emma
reflected, walking across the lawn in obedience to
the commanding tone. 'My dear your friend here
has been waiting for you for the last ten minutes.'

Robert? Emma screwed her eyes up against the
harsh dazzle of the sun, all the colour leaving her
face as she found herself meeting the implaccable
gaze of Drake Harwood.

'Emma, darling . . .'

Quite how she came to be in his arms, Emma
wasn't sure, but what she did know was that his
arms constricted her body like a steel vice, making
sure there was no escape. His breath, clean and
fresh, brought goosebumps up under her skin, her
lips parting in instant protest as she tensed her
body furiously against him.

'Sweetheart, you look entrancing.' He said the
words loud enough for the half dozen or so people
standing close by to hear, and they numbered
among them the photographer from the local
newspaper who was covering the event for them,
Emma noticed tensely as she tried to fight off an
overwhelming feeling of disbelief. This could not
be happening. She could not be here in Dr ke
Harwood's arms, her palms pressed flat against his
chest, feeling the steady beat of his heart.

'Kiss me . . .' He made the command against her
lips, the words soundless.

Rage and rejection mingled hotly in Emma's eyes as she tried to force him away, but the moment she opened her mouth to demand that he release her it was captured by his.

His lips were warm and firm, skilled in the way they moved over hers, leaving tiny tremors of pleasure feathering over her skin. Hardly able to believe her response to him, Emma shivered in reaction. Of course she had not responded to him ... but her mouth tingled from his kiss as he released her, and his eyes mocked her as she cringed away.

'Emma my dear, what a dark horse you are ...' Mrs T. sounded both chagrined and excited. 'Why on earth didn't you tell us.'

Tell them what Emma thought numbly? What on earth had Drake Harwood said to her? Certainly he couldn't have revealed the fact that she had posed naked for his magazine ... there was far too much awe in Mrs T's voice for that.

'Emma didn't want to steal her sister's limelight ... did you my pet?'

The hard grip on her arm warned her against rebellion, the smooth voice coating an intent resolve revealed to her by the cold gleam in dark green eyes.

'Emma?' That was Camilla's voice sharp with anxiety and anger. 'What's going on?'

'I ...'

'Emma was just about to tell me off for letting the cat out of the bag about our engagement,' Drake Harwood intervened smoothly. 'Weren't you darling?'

She simply did not know what to say. She felt as though she had strayed into a make-believe world

where nothing made sense. What on earth was
Drake Harwood talking about? What was the
purpose of his ridiculous announcement? She
couldn't understand any of it. She opened her
mouth to contradict his statement and then fell
silent as he said softly to the hovering photographer. 'I hope you've taken some of Emma . . .
she's most photogenic. I have some quite
spectacular shots of her, haven't I darling?'

He was threatening her, damn him, reminding
her of the hold he had over her. She could just
imagine Mrs T's face if he were to reveal now just
what those photographs were and how he intended
to use them.

She could see Camilla looking anxiously from
Drake to herself. She came towards them, a fixed
smile on her face, David at her side. Before Emma
could intervene Drake was speaking, smiling
pleasantly as he greeted her sister. 'Hello Camilla.
What a beautiful bride you make, and this of
course, must be . . .'

'David.' Camilla supplied in a tight, bitter voice.
The glance she darted at Emma spoke volumes,
and Emma was tempted to tell her that Drake's
presence was none of her doing.

Emma could see that David was frowning
slightly as he looked at Camilla. David possessed a
deeply jealous streak which rarely surfaced, but
when it did . . .

Camilla too had seen the look. 'I met Drake the
last time I was in London, darling.' She was
babbling tensely, and Emma had the uneasy
sensation that David was none too pleased by this
disclosure.

'Yes, it is thanks to your wife that I got to know

Emma,' Drake intervened. If she hadn't known him better she might almost have thought he was deliberately trying to reassure David, Emma thought cynically, but Drake Harwood had not struck her as a man who would put himself out for another human being unless he stood to gain something from doing so.

'Come on darling, I want to thank Uncle Ted for standing in for Daddy.' Camilla tugged tensely at David's arm, and he allowed himself to be led away.

Before she could take Drake to task Mrs T. bore down on them, beaming fulsomely, and Emma groaned inwardly, knowing it would be quite some time before they could escape.

CHAPTER FOUR

As Emma had suspected it was a good fifteen minutes before Mrs T. left, but the moment she could, she steered Drake out of earshot of the other guests and rounded on him, her eyes blazing as she demanded fiercely, 'And just what was all that about?'

'All what?'

He was laughing at her, damn him. Mentally grinding her teeth and trying to hold on to her temper, Emma said quietly, 'You know exactly what I mean, so don't pretend you don't ... I'm talking about the way you are giving the impression that you and I are ...' she struggled for words.

While she hesitated, Drake cut in smoothly, 'Are more than just good friends?' He smiled sardonically. 'We can't have the discussion you're obviously itching to have here; we'll discuss the whole thing over dinner tonight. I've booked us a table at the George ... I'm staying there for the whole weekend.'

His high-handedness robbed her of the breath to expostulate, and by the time she had regained it it was too late; her father was almost level with them, Uncle Ted in tow.

'Ah Emma, there you are ...' he smiled his usual vague smile at her, 'and this must be the young man Mrs T. has been telling me about.'

As Drake shook the vicar's extended hand,

Emma was struck anew by the leashed virility of him; the sensation of male power, so intensely heightened by her father's frailer more aesthetic appearance.

'I believe you're something of a name in financial circles,' he added conversationally.

The three men chatted for several minutes, and Emma was surprised to learn that Drake too had been up at Oxford, although not at her father's college. When Uncle Ted started describing at length the bad luck he had had with his shares, Emma judged it was time for them to move away. She could sense her father's quizzical speculation, and knew that he was wondering why Drake had never been brought into any of their conversations.

The vicar was a liberal, if somewhat vague, father, always inclined to take a distant and global view of any given situation and there was no earthly reason why, if Emma had genuinely been as involved with Drake as he was pretending, she would not have mentioned him to her parent.

The afternoon seemed to drag on interminably; Emma could scarcely touch her food, delicious though she was sure it was. The several glasses of champagne she consumed helped to steady her over-wrought nerves but they couldn't stop her from fuming inwardly every time she thought of Drake's high-handed behaviour. How dare he come down here and interfere with her life. What did he want from her anyway?

After the reception she had to go back to the house with Camilla to help her change. The moment the bedroom door closed behind them her sister turned on her, her pretty face flushed and angry as she demanded. 'What is he doing here? Emma how could you invite him. You know. . .'

'Just a minute, I didn't invite him, Mrs T. did. Somehow he managed to convince her that he and I are . . . "good friends".' Emma gritted her teeth over the last two words. 'I had no idea that he was going to turn up here, and I still don't know why he did . . .'

She didn't know, but she suspected it must have something to do with the fact that she had not accepted the television job. Initially she had expected a reaction from him but when weeks had gone by without one, she had decided that he had accepted that there was nothing he could do.

'David wanted to know where I'd met him. I'm sure he suspects something,' Camilla told her fretfully. 'Why did he have to come down here?'

'If you told David the truth it would save us both a lot of problems,' Emma responded astringently. 'Honestly Camilla, you're storing up a lot of trouble for yourself by not doing so. If I were you . . .'

'But you're not are you,' Camilla snapped. 'I suppose you couldn't resist encouraging him. After all it's not every day you get to meet a man like Drake Harwood. Well I'm warning you Em . . . he changes his girls like most men change their underwear, and you'll have some pretty stiff competition. I can't think what he sees in you,' she added tactlessly, 'he normally goes for the glamorous type; model girls, actresses. . .' Her expression changed as she stared into the mirror, a preening, self-satisfied look that Emma was familiar with, chasing the petulance out of her face. 'Of course . . . why didn't I think of it before

. . . I expect he's just using you as an excuse to see me.'

'On your wedding day?' Emma asked drily, suddenly and for no reason that she could think of, so angry with her sister that she wanted to slap her. 'Come on Camilla . . .'

'You're just jealous.' Camilla whirled round to face her, two angry spots of colour burning in her cheeks. 'You've always been jealous of me . . . that's why you want me to tell David, so that it will make trouble between us. Well I'm telling you now Emma, that a man like Drake Harwood wouldn't look twice at you, if you weren't my sister. He wants *me* all right. I'm sure of it, and he's come down here today to let me know it. He doesn't want to get married, everyone knows that, and I expect he thinks that now that I'm married . . .'

'The two of you can indulge in an affair without anyone being the wiser. . . You might have a pretty face Camilla,' she told her sister shortly, 'but you've got an empty brain and a cold heart. I don't envy you . . . I feel sorry for you.'

She walked out before she said anything more she might regret. Let Camilla finish changing by herself. If she had to stay with her sister a moment longer, she could not be responsible for her actions. She passed David on the stairs, already changed into casual slacks shirt and jacket. He caught her arm as she passed him, frowning slightly.

'Em about this Drake Harwood chap . . . Just how well does Camilla know him?'

She was tired of shielding Camilla, she thought bitterly, tired of always having to put her first.

'Why don't you ask her that yourself David?' she suggested curtly. 'I . . .'

'So there you are darling . . . I was just coming to see if I could find you.'

Hard fingers circled her wrist, cool green eyes studying her flushed cheeks and angry eyes. 'I've barely been gone half an hour,' she said tersely, caught completely off her guard when Drake transferred his grip from her wrist to her waist, pulling her firmly into his arms, despite David's presence, his body hard and firm against hers, as his unexpected action caused her to fall heavily against him, her breath tangling in her throat.

'That's twenty-five minutes too long.' His free hand moved against her nape, the words feathered across her forehead.

Emma was aware of David muttering something about having to go, and hurrying past them. It must have been the jolt to her system of finding herself so suddenly off balance that was playing havoc with her pulses, she thought faintly, trying to stem the flooding tide of weakness flowing through her. There was a dangerous enchantment in being held like this . . . in being wrapped in concern; in being cosseted and cared for by strong male arms.

With a jerk Emma brought her thoughts under control. What was the matter with her; was she losing her mind? How could she possibly believe even for a second that Drake Harwood's arms offered security and warmth? He was merely acting a part . . . merely pretending to care about her . . . although as yet she did not know why.

'Let me go.' She pushed a bunched up fist against his chest, trying to reinforce her plea with physical force, but trying to match her strength against his was laughable. Indeed he was laughing; she could feel the sound rumbling deep in his chest, and when she raised her eyes to meet his, they were a dense dark green; gleaming with mockery and amusement.

That he should dare to laugh at her was like a lighted match applied to the fuse paper of her temper; badly frayed during the build up to the wedding, her taut nerves suddenly seemed unable to take any more.

'Don't you dare laugh at me,' she told him tensely. 'Just what. . .?'

'Why did you refuse to take the television job?'

His eyes weren't amused any longer; they were cold and watchful, the crisp question taking the heat out of her anger; confusing her almost. Her mouth compressed into a firm line. She didn't have to answer his questions; let him answer them himself.

'Not going to speak? Well I know a remedy for that . . .'

Before she knew what he was doing Emma felt the warm pressure of his mouth on hers; not painfully or brutally—that she could have dealt with. No, his lips were caressing hers with a mobile, experienced sensuality that made her pulses jerk into confused awareness and her heart pound as idiotically as a gullible teenager's. It made no sense; there was no logical reason that she could think of why he should be able to arouse this reaction inside her; her intelligence told her that experience alone could not be the answer.

What he was doing to her was a true seduction of the senses, she thought hazily; he was using his

skill and her vulnerability as a weapon against her
and it was one which he wielded with deadly
accuracy. His tongue, warm and knowing, stroked
along the curves of her still closed mouth,
investigating the tensely held in corners, urging her
body without using words, to disobey the
commands of her brain. The scrape of his teeth
against her lower lip was intensely erotic; so much
so that she trembled visibly; knowing that if she
didn't give in she would soon be swamped with
sensations she would not be able to control.

Against his chest the hands she had curled into
fists uncurled and pressed flat as she tried to push
him away. Her neck felt as though it was going to
snap beneath the pressure he was applying to her
nape to keep her mouth still under his, but from
somewhere she found the strength to pull away
just enough to mutter thickly, 'All right, all right
. . . I'll tell you . . .'

His eyes were incredibly dark, she realised as her
own locked with them; dark and hot; burning with
an intensity that poured rivers of heat under her
own skin. She had thought he was simply cold
bloodedly trying to dominate her, but the heat of
his concentrated study told a different story.

'Too late . . .' The sound of the words
reverberated against her mouth as his own possessed
it, hotly and deeply, his hand at her nape, curling
into her hair and bending her back until her body
was as taut as a bow string, her breasts pressed flat
against his chest, her mouth vulnerable to any assault
he chose to make on it. She had to grip his shoulders
to stop herself from overbalancing; her senses
rioting out of control, her mouth warm and pliant
beneath his, betraying her commands in favour of

response to a deep rooted need that seemed to have sprung up inside her.

He ended the kiss slowly, lingering over his enjoyment of it, rubbing his thumb softly over the swollen contours of her mouth as he released her.

His eyes were almost jade green; hot as a tropical night, almost smothering her in a sensation of heat and languor.

'Now tell me,' he murmured as she stepped unsteadily away from him. 'Why did you refuse to take the job?'

'Did you expect me to do anything different?' Now that she was free and back in control of her own body an irrational feverish anger possessed her; that most of the anger should have been directed against herself Emma couldn't deny; he hadn't forced a response from her, she acknowledged; he had seduced it; and she fool that she was had responded to that seduction. Her heart was still pounding as though she had been running; her skin hot and prickly. She wanted to deny the effect he had had on her but it was there in the aching tension in the pit of her stomach and the shivering bewilderment of her body.

'How could I take it?' she stormed on, trying to ignore the vulnerability he had revealed to her, and which she had never suspected herself capable of. 'How could I sign a contract, knowing what you intended to do. . .?'

'So instead you cheated on our bargain, by refusing the job, believing that I wouldn't use the photographs if you weren't employed by the studio?'

He was watching her closely, but Emma was too angry to pay much attention.

'No!' she told him vehemently. 'It wasn't like
that at all. You can do what you like with them
. . . humiliate *me* as much as you care to . . . but it
will just be *me* you humiliate, not Emma Court
Newsreader, I won't be manipulated in that. I
won't be used in your publicity war against a rival
magazine . . .'

'And your present job?' He said it quietly, still
watching her and Emma had the distinct impression that he already knew.

'I've handed in my notice.'

'So at the present time you're out of a job. . .'

'That's right . . . but no doubt I'll be offered
plenty once your magazine comes out . . .
When. . .?' Her throat closed up and she had to
swallow hard to appear unconcerned as she asked
coolly, 'When will my photographs appear?'

'That's up to you.' He was watching her
carefully, 'But it isn't something I care to discuss
right now. We'll talk about it tonight. You've
surprised me you know,' he told her as he stepped
away from her and down the stairs, and the way
he said it told Emma that he wasn't used to being
surprised by her sex. 'Nine of ten women would
have signed that contract and left others to cope
with the ensuing uproar. . .'

'Then it's no doubt unfortunate for us both that
I happen to be the tenth isn't it?' Emma said
tautly. She heard footsteps on the stairs behind her
and glanced up to see Camilla coming down. Her
sister ignored her, and instead smiled at Drake,
dimpling him a flirtatious smile.

'Drake, you are very naughty, turning up like
this,' she teased, linking her arm with his. 'Poor
David is terribly jealous.'

'Is he?' Emma could have sworn there was derision and even faint contempt in the green eyes as they rested on her sister's face. 'Have you told him what happened yet?'

Flirtatiousness gave way to alarm as Camilla withdrew from him. 'No ... and neither must you,' she exclaimed hurriedly. 'Promise you won't. . .'

'I've already given that promise—to your sister,' Drake said coolly ... 'We struck a bargain over it, and I've no intention of reneging on my side of it ...' His eyes met Emma's over Camilla's head. 'I'll pick you up for our dinner date at seven,' he said to Emma, and there was a warning implicit in the words that told her she would be unwise to try to evade him.

It was just gone six and Emma had just reached home. Her father and Uncle Ted were closeted in the study, reminiscing, and perfectly content with one another's company. As she turned to go up the stairs Emma tried to control her erratic pulses. Dinner with Drake. . . If only she didn't have to go. She was behaving like a gauche adolescent, she scorned herself; where was her self-control; her poise? Neither had proved inviolate.

She had lost them when Drake kissed her, she acknowledged wryly. In retrospect it seemed impossible that a mere kiss should have such a devastating effect on her, and she was inclined to think she had overreacted; something brought on by her quarrel with Camilla and the stresses and strains leading up to the wedding. It seemed a much more plausible explanation than to admit that sexually at least she found Drake Harwood

overwhelmingly attractive. That she could respond
to someone so intensely on a purely sexual level,
had been something she had never considered or
experienced before, and it was a touch disconcert-
ing.

She dressed for their dinner date almost
automatically. Her wardrobe wasn't extensive;
unlike Camilla she wasn't a clothes-aholic and she
pondered on what to wear, ultimately selecting a
new Caroline Charles outfit she had purchased in
a fit of extravagance. The slim black silk skirt
clung to her hips, the white jacket cut to mould
itself neatly to her body emphasising her narrow
waist. The jacket buttoned at a military angle and
although simple, the outfit could be dressed up or
down as the occasion demanded. Black silk
stockings and high heeled shoes completed the
outfit, and after scrutinising herself carefully in her
mirror Emma decided that she had chosen
correctly. The plain black and white of her suit
gave off a formal, even faintly austere impression
she decided, not seeing in the way the silk clung to
her body a sensuality that was not immediately
obvious but which held an allure that would linger
long after the more obvious had been forgotten.

Drake arrived exactly on the dot of seven. She
heard the Ferrari long before she saw it. Monster,
she thought tetchily, glancing out of her bedroom
window, as it stopped outside. A bright gleaming
red, it certainly caught the eye, she decided
cynically—exactly right for the type of man who
liked to be noticed; to cause a ripple of interest
when he appeared.

She dodged back away from the window, as
Drake got out and walked up the path. She was in

the hall by the time he rang the bell, opening the door to him with cool pleasantness. That was the best way to treat him she had decided, with a certain amount of tolerant disdain.

He raised his eyebrows as he studied her and pronounced, 'Very nice . . . In fact very, very nice.'

For some reason his compliment angered her. She felt like rushing upstairs and ripping the suit off. *That* was it, she decided as she gave him a cool smile, it was his air of believing that she had dressed specifically to please and attract *him* that infuriated her; that and his lordly bestowal of the compliment—a bone for a trained performing dog, she thought waspishly, following him out to his car.

Contrary to her expectations he was a controlled and considerate driver. Almost as though he realised her disdain for his car, he flicked a glance at her as he drove and said whimsically, 'This car is the embodiment of all my boyhood dreams—it's something of an anachronism in these days of petrol shortages and fuel conserving cars, but . . .' He shrugged and then added, 'I sense a certain amount of disapproval. Is it for the car . . . or for me?'

'A car is an inanimate object,' Emma responded coolly.

'Ah, so it is for me . . .'

'You can hardly expect me to be thrilled by the way you've turned up out of the blue and forced this dinner date on me,' Emma told him.

'But surely you expected some response? You must have known I wouldn't let your actions go by unremarked upon?'

'I didn't do it as an attention seeking exercise,' Emma told him curtly, infuriated by the intimation

behind his words that she had deliberately set out
to entice a response from him. 'I did it because my
own code of ethics prevented me from taking the
job when I knew that by doing so I would be
causing a good deal of potential embarrassment to
my employers . . .'

'Yes. It's very strong, isn't it, this code of ethics
of your yours? First it leads you into protecting your
sister, and then to protecting your would-be
employers. I wonder if it could be extended to
embrace me as well.'

'You?' Emma turned scornful eyes toward him.
'And what would you need to be protected from?'

'Oh you'd be surprised,' he told her softly,
forestalling any further questions by adding, 'but
we'll discuss it over dinner. Here we are . . .' As
he turned into the George's narrow car-park
entrance, Emma fell silent so that he could
concentrate on manoeuvring the car. He parked it
deftly and then helped her to alight. He had all the
old-fashioned gentlemanly courtesies at his finger-
tips she had to give him that . . . but that didn't
change the fact that he was still a wolf . . . and as
rapacious and dangerous as any of that breed,
despite any sheep's clothing he might choose to
assume.

Emma could tell by the deference of the waiters
that they, like her, were aware of his aura of power
and self-confidence. Their table was slightly
secluded from the others; by a window, which in the
already fading daylight gave pleasant views over the
George's garden. Once an old-fashioned coaching
inn, the hotel had gardens which stretched down to
the river, and in summer the restaurant was often
packed with out of town visitors who had heard of

its charm and excellent chef.

'Well,' Emma pounced the moment they had given their order. 'What do you want to talk to me about that couldn't be said this afternoon.'

'Let's eat first.' His lazy drawl, and the laconic way he smiled at her increased Emma's impotent fury. He seemed determined to reinforce the fact that *he* was the one in control; that he held the whip handle. 'If you pick a fight with me now it will only ruin your digestion,' he added accurately reading the intention in her tense posture. What was it about this man that drove her beyond the limits of all reasonable caution; that practically willed her to behave in a way that was in direct contradiction of the standards she normally set herself?

'I don't have the slightest intention of picking a fight with you,' she lied coldly. 'I'm not a child Drake; and besides,' she added tauntingly, 'what makes you think you're so immune?'

She had wanted to prick his ego a little, to bring home to him the fact that he too was only human, but all he did was laugh and say lazily, 'Discipline ... I'm a very disciplined man, Emma. I never waste either time or energy if I can help it. Unlike you I have no desire to fight ... on the contrary ...'

The look he gave her reminded Emma forcibly of the way he had kissed her on the stairs that afternoon. A warm, golden heat slithered disturbingly along her veins, but she forced herself to ignore it, to ignore everything but the food in front of her. Disciplined was he, she thought bitterly, glancing surreptitiously at him. Well she should show him what discipline was.

It was torture not to demand that he tell her exactly why he had sought her out, and by the time they had reached the coffee stage of their meal Emma was ready to burst with ire and impatience.

Even so she was determined not to say a word. She would wait for him to speak.

He had been served with a brandy before he did so, Emma having refused a liqueur. She had already drunk quite enough for one day, what with the champagne this afternoon and now wine with her meal. Something told her that she was going to need her wits about her to contend with Drake Harwood successfully.

Her self-control, hard won though it had been, hadn't deceived him. He smiled at her as he warmed his brandy glass in his palm and remarked softly, 'Very well done Emma... You know I find myself admiring you more and more all the time.'

'Then don't,' Emma said shortly. 'Save your admiration for those who want it.'

'Like your silly little sister, do you mean. You know,' he ruminated slowly, 'I'm surprised at her new husband, he'd have been much better off with you.'

'David happens to love Camilla,' Emma told him stiffly. Despite her own doubts concerning the marriage, she wasn't going to let anyone else get away with such a provocative statement, especially when it implied a criticism of her sister.

'I hope to God he isn't expecting a virgin bride.'

The comment stunned her.

'Oh come on,' he was patently amused, 'don't tell me you can't see that he's the type who would, but unlike you my dear, Camilla is anything but virgin. And no, I'm not speaking from personal experience,' he added laconically before she could say a word, 'but certain things speak for themselves, and just as there is that about you that tells me that you have had no lover; there is that about your sister that tells me she has.'

Emma thought of several retorts and banished them all in favour of what she hoped was a coldly repressive silence.

'What's the matter? Shocked because I've guessed the truth? Are you really so ashamed of it, Emma?'

'Neither ashamed or proud,' she told him with a coolness she was very proud of. Some deep seated instinct warned her against lying; he would know immediately what she was doing and it would be humiliating to be taxed with *that* on top of everything else. 'It is simply that as yet I have not met . . .'

'Met a man you want to go to bed with,' Drake finished for her. He was regarding her with open amusement. 'At least you hadn't, until recently isn't that it, Emma?'

His audacity took her breath away. Too intelligent to pretend she didn't know what he meant, Emma fought down the angry tide of colour threatening to run up under her skin and said freezingly, 'Your ego must be mammoth Drake. Believe me I have no desire whatsoever to . . .'

'Go to bed with me?' He said it for her, laughing openly at her expression.

On the verge of reinforcing his statement with a heated denial Emma decided to show more

caution. She shrugged aside his comment with
what she hoped was aplomb and said instead.
'Look, why did you want to see me. . .? Was it to
tell me when the photographs will appear?'

'Only sort of.' He pushed aside his brandy glass
and leaned towards her, watching her carefully, all
evidence of his earlier bantering mockery gone. 'I
have a proposition to put to you Emma. Let me
explain it to you if you will before you make any
comments. Now, are you ready?'

When she nodded her head mutely he said.
'Very well. As you may know the magazine came
into my hands as part of a package when I took
over its controlling parent. It hasn't been doing all
that well and I confess that initially I thought it
might be worthwhile trying to boost circulation
but now I'm having second thoughts. For the most
part my business interests lie in a different field.'
He paused and looked across at her. 'At the
present time I'm in negotiation to sell off the
magazine to someone else. Negotiations have
reached a very delicate stage. He wants the
magazine but he's not prepared to meet my price
or terms, and I'm not prepared to sell until he
does. Most importantly I want to ensure security
for all the staff on the magazine before I sign
anything, and that's proving something of a
sticking point.

'My prospective purchaser is an American, I
met him and his wife last year while I was in the
States—although she wasn't his wife then.'

Something in the way he said it alerted Emma,
unable to keep silent she asked waspishly, 'What
was she then—your girlfriend?'

'Something like that . . . Let's just say we were . . .

good friends. However, Giles was prepared to offer marriage and I wasn't, so Bianca married him.'

He glanced down at the table and frowned. 'Giles is an extremely jealous husband ... very much older than Bianca too. It appears that she is very keen to resume the relationship we once had ... I, on the other hand feel that it would be extremely unwise to do so, especially if I want to exact the best possible terms I can from Giles.'

'Yes indeed,' Emma agreed sardonically. 'I can quite see that he wouldn't be inclined to be particularly generous if he found out that you'd been having an affair with his wife, but I can't see what all this has to do with me?'

'Can't you?' He smiled wolfishly at her, 'Then perhaps I'd better explain. Bianca is threatening to blackmail me into resuming our relationship by revealing to Giles that we were once lovers. If he knows that he will immediately assume that I still want her. He's that sort of man, and almost obsessed with Bianca to the extent that in his eyes she can do no wrong, so I thought I might try a little blackmail myself ...'

Emma didn't know what he meant, but cold fingers touched her skin as she looked into his eyes.

'If I promise not to publish those photographs of you Emma, would you agree to pose as my fiancée for the duration of their visit?'

Her first instinctive question of 'but why ask me. .?' was answered immediately by her own senses, a cynical smile curving her mouth as she answered herself. 'But of course ... with me you won't have the additional worry of being blackmailed into a genuine marriage by your fake fiancée.'

'Very astute,' Drake agreed. 'That was something that taxed my mind when I first decided a
fiancée was what I needed to keep Bianca at bay
and Giles . . .'

'Unsuspicious?' Emma supplied contemptuously.
'I won't do it Drake,' she told him, making to get up,
but he grasped her wrist as she did so and forced her
to regain her seat. 'I thought you might say that,' he
drawled easily, 'but my dear have you really thought
the whole thing through? Already your family and
friends know you're involved with me. Once those
photographs are published they'll assume that
we've been lovers and that I've dumped you. This
way at least you can have the satisfaction of
ridding yourself of *me* when the charade is over.
Besides, I can hardly believe that either your father
or your new brother-in-law would relish the
thought of you appearing in . . .'

He had her in a corner and he knew it Emma
thought bitterly. She could see no way out. This
man was a master when it came to manipulating
people. But he couldn't succeed in controlling his
ex-mistress, she thought, so he wasn't completely
invulnerable.

'Well?'

'I don't have much choice do I?' Emma said
tautly. It would be a relief to know that those
photographs of her would never be published.
Could she trust him in that regard? Instinct told
her that she could. They were of scant use to him
now and would be of even less value once he had
sold the magazine. She could hardly think that this
Giles whoever he was would be remotely interested
in half a dozen or so shots of some English girl no
one had ever heard of.

'Not really.' His smile was amused and that amusement stung Emma's pride.

Lifting her head challengingly she said, 'There is just one thing though—won't your ... friend ... think it strange that you're engaged to me?'

When he looked blank, she added acidly, 'After all I'm scarcely up to your usual high standard of glamour ... and of course, as you remarked yourself earlier, I am still a virgin.'

As she watched the skin tighten over his facial bones Emma knew she had made a dangerous mistake.

'Luckily for you Bianca isn't all that astute where her own sex is concerned. She sees what she wants to see. Don't try needling me Emma,' he warned her drily as the waiter brought their bill, 'you might not like the results.'

CHAPTER FIVE

ONCE he had set his mind on a course, Drake obviously pursued it with a single mindedness that confirmed his adherence to discipline Emma reflected, staring bleakly at the elegant, solitaire diamond ring glittering on her left hand. He had arrived with it this morning, having spoken to her on the telephone the previous evening to warn her of his arrival.

It was just over a week since the wedding and she hadn't seen him once during that period although he had rung her every day. Emma had known that her father was waiting for her to say something; to mention Drake's presence in her life, and at last, last night knowing it could not be put off any longer she had gone to him and told him that she and Drake were getting engaged.

'I didn't want to say anything before because I didn't want to steal Camilla's thunder,' she had told him awkwardly, hating the lie and the man who had made it necessary.

A little to her surprise her father had accepted her explanation quite easily. 'You won't want a long engagement I don't expect, and to judge from what I've seen of him, neither will your young man. You always did have a good deal more fire beneath the surface than most people give you credit for, Emma,' he had added, further surprising her and making her tense in remembered shock as she recalled how her body had leapt with sexual excitement when Drake touched her.

She could only pray that their engagement was of short duration. She wished she could appear totally indifferent to him, because she sensed that her rage against her response to him amused him, and she would not put it past him to deliberately encourage it because he was amused by her reaction. Now she knew how a wild animal felt when it was caught in a trap she reflected, pretending she was studying the awesome glitter of her ring, while in reality what she was doing was avoiding the speculative curiosity in Drake's eyes.

He had arrived just under an hour ago, and with an old fashioned courtesy she thought both unnecessary and overdone in the circumstances, had insisted on speaking privately with her father.

When they had emerged from his study both men had been laughing. Her father wouldn't laugh if he knew the truth Emma thought angrily, but then neither would he automatically blame Drake—that wasn't his way. He would have to analyse and consider the situation before apportioning blame. She sighed fretfully, wishing for once she might have a less objective and more emotional parent. A lot of people thought she was like him, coolly weighing the pros and cons of a situation before acting, but in reality she was not. She had only learned through bitter mistakes to force herself to do so, to take the long cool view of things before reacting.

For the first time in years Emma turned her keen intelligence inwards on herself and was mildly shocked to discover how long she'd been playing a part; been adopting a character that wasn't really

hers . . . or at least was only in part hers. In two
short interviews Drake Harwood had stripped
away far too much of that adopted character, to
reveal the passionate intense woman who hid
behind it, and Emma suddenly felt thoroughly
frightened by that discovery.

It was the searching intensity of his glance,
rather than his words that brought her out of her
reverie, but she stood stock still, tense with the
shock of knowing he was about to deliver another
blow as she heard him saying. 'Yes . . . it is rather
a nuisance. I'd have preferred them to come over
here, but he's insisting that I go there, and since
he's the piper in this case I'm afraid I'll have to
pay the tune. We'll only be gone a fortnight or so
though . . .'

Gone? Gone where? He must have read the
question in her eyes before she could voice it,
because he turned towards her and said mildly, 'I
was just telling your father, darling, that we won't
have time for an engagement celebration because
we have to leave for New York at the end of the
week. Giles has too many business commitments
to leave the States right now and Bianca has very
kindly suggested that we can stay with them for
the duration of our visit . . .'

Caution warned Emma to wait until they were
alone to question him. She went through the ritual
of having a celebratory drink with her father and
Drake in an angry state of tension. Why had
Drake changed his plans, and why hadn't he
consulted her first?

'If you'll excuse us, I'd like to take my new
fiancée out to lunch,' Drake said at length,
standing up. Emma rose automatically herself,

flinching with barely concealed temper as Drake put out a hand to touch her arm, very much the solicitous fiancé. She hated him touching her, she boiled inwardly, she hated this deceit she had been forced to enter into ... she ... red hot darts of awareness arrowed along her nervous system from the point of contact with his hand. She badly wanted to pull away, but with her father looking on it was impossible.

The lunch date had been arranged before Drake arrived, to give them an opportunity or so Emma had thought to finalise the arrangements for Giles and Bianca's arrival. She had already half prepared her father for her absence.

A realist and comparatively broad-minded, she knew he would make no objection from a moral point of view, but there was still the smooth running of the parish and the vicarage to consider and with this in mind Emma had engaged Mrs Johnson, who came in occasionally to help them out, on a full-time basis.

Emma got into Drake's car in a stony, angry silence, not speaking, not wanting to speak until she could trust herself not to let her rage boil over and swamp her.

When she felt she had some measure of self-control she turned to him and said coolly. 'What's all this about our going to New York?'

'Bianca's decision,' Drake told her tersely. 'So don't go thinking it's some clever plan of mine. I suppose I ought to have expected it. Bianca's a master tactician and knows as well as I do the advantage of being on one's home ground so to speak. I'll warn you now she'll try everything she can to cause trouble between us.'

'She knows about our engagement then?' Emma spoke cynically. 'What a brave man you are Drake, hiding behind a woman's skirts.'

'On the contrary,' he told her drily, 'I prefer to consider it as fighting fire with fire. Besides, Bianca on her own I can handle. . .'

'By doing what? Going to bed with her? But of course you can't do that with her husband around and likely to find out can you?'

'Snappy this morning aren't we?' he commented laconically. 'You know you're a better actress than I thought, for a moment you almost managed to inject a tinge of jealousy into your voice. Keep that up and Bianca will be in no doubt as to the reality of our relationship.'

For a moment Emma was too furious to respond. She *had* been jealous she realised on a wave of self-contempt, bitterly, hotly jealous; imagining him making love to the unknown Bianca.

'All she has to do is to tell her husband that you and she were once lovers,' Emma reminded him.

'She won't do that . . . Giles is a very wealthy man. No, what Bianca wants is the sense of power that being able to force me to do what she wants gives her. A lot of women are like that although they cloak their greed for power in other emotions . . . usually fake. Mind you, I suspect that Bianca hasn't given up completely.'

'How very flattering for you,' Emma commented waspishly. 'What am I supposed to do about it? Lie outside your bedroom door like a devoted guard?'

'Would you?' A wicked grin slashed across his face, his eyes sparkling deeply green as he glanced at her. 'Of course there is an even better way you could protect me . . .'

Watching her frown, he said softly, 'You could share my bed.' Her body tensed automatically and obviously, and Drake's derisive laughter grated across sensitive nerves. 'Don't worry my little virgin. I'm not about to demand the ultimate sacrifice.'

'Don't *you* worry,' Emma snapped back, through closed teeth. 'Because you aren't about to get it.'

Drake's rich chuckle worried her, but she strove to hide her anxiety from him. It sounded so lighthearted . . . and . . . and self-confident, she thought anxiously, almost as though he knew quite well just how easy it would be for her to abandon the moral code she had lived her life by and slake herself with almost feverish greed on the purely physical pleasure his body could offer hers. And that's all it was; simply a physical need that he brought to life inside her. Deep, strong and very intense, but completely without any finer feelings or emotions to temper it.

Perhaps that was why it was so strong, Emma pondered inwardly; perhaps like a weed it needed no nourishment to grow, as love and caring did. She was shaken by the thought, shaken and cautious, so much so that she kept quiet during their meal, speaking only in monosyllables until Drake raised his eyebrows and said mockingly, 'What's the matter? Surely you aren't frightened?'

That depended, Emma thought bitterly to herself. Certainly she was frightened of the feelings he aroused inside her, what sane person would not be?

'Of Bianca or of you?' she asked coolly. 'I'm not a fool Drake. Of course I'm frightened. Most people are when they're confronted by ruthlessness so intense and self-motivated that it smashes everything in its path. I should have thought you and Bianca would be well suited. So far everything you've told me about her makes me think she's possibly the only woman alive who'd be a match for you.'

'You think so?' The smile he gave her sent prickles of awareness shivering along her spine. 'Well there are matches and matches. However, when the time comes for me to settle down it won't be with a woman of Bianca's calibre. By the way,' he added briskly, 'before we leave I want you to come and spend a couple of days in London. I've booked you into the Inn on the Park. You'll need some new clothes . . . a new hair-do perhaps, and . . .'

The way he was studying her made Emma itch to hit him. 'I'm sorry if my looks, my clothes and my hair, don't meet your exacting standards,' she told him seethingly, 'but they suit me, and I won't change them and furthermore if they don't suit you then I suggest you go and look somewhere else for your bogus fiancée.'

'Temper, temper.' His voice was mild, but his eyes so totally amused that Emma longed to throw something at him. 'I didn't say they didn't suit me,' he told her eyeing her in a way that made her skin tense over her bones and her muscles ache. 'Personally I can't think of any way I'd rather see you than without any clothes at all and all that glorious red hair spread out around you on my pillow . . . but it was you I was thinking of. New clothes, a new hairstyle, they all help to give a woman confidence—armour if you like . . .'

'And I'm going to need it against Bianca aren't I?' Emma murmured, seeing the sense of his words, and too anxious to forget the images his earlier ones had conjured up to take him too much to task. There had been a photograph very like the mental picture he had just painted of her among the batch Pat had taken and her skin crawled in revulsion as she thought about him looking at it . . . studying her naked body . . .

'No, I didn't,' he said calmly breaking into her thoughts. For a moment Emma simply looked blankly at him. 'I didn't look at the proofs Pat sent to me. They're locked in my safe in the same envelope they came to me in.'

'Insurance against my good behaviour,' Emma said bitterly, not wanting him to see how relieved she was. 'I'm surprised you don't know each one off by heart.'

It was an inflammatory thing to say, and it was born of her own aching humiliation that they had been taken at all.

'I'm no voyeur, Emma,' he told her curtly, 'we both know that if I wanted to see your naked body, it would be relatively easy for me to see— and touch—the real thing. Stop taking what happened so personally. It wasn't. At that time I was hoping to boost the magazine's circulation. You arrived opportunely—for me, and had you taken that job I should have published the photographs perhaps three or four months from now, when your face was known, and who knows I might have found the magazine profitable enough to retain. As it is . . .' he shrugged and added warningly, 'Don't push me too hard. Some allowances I am prepared to make, but you fight every inch of the way don't you?'

Too stunned by his comment about seeing and touching her, Emma could only marshal her thoughts sufficiently to say bitterly, 'Commodities, that's all people are to you isn't it? You don't give a damn about their feelings.'

'Perhaps because the people I'm dealing with don't give a damn about mine, and you're wrong you know. I cared enough about yours to employ—at considerable expense I might add—a woman photographer. I could simply have sent you along to the sort of studio my rival uses—but I didn't, did I?' he said grimly.

What he was saying was true. Emma remembered how relieved she had been when she saw Pat but her pride ached too much for her to acknowledge the truth of his comment.

'Stop worrying about it,' he told her curtly. 'Once this is over and the magazine is sold, you can burn the damn things and forget all about it.'

'I might be able to burn them,' Emma told him in a voice taut with self-loathing, 'but how can I burn my memories, how can I forget. . .?'

'There are times when we all have to do things we don't want to,' Drake cut in harshly. He had gone curiously pale and Emma wondered if perhaps he cared more about Bianca than he was letting her see. It seemed curious to her that a man as strong and hard as this one couldn't cope with an importuning woman. Perhaps he was frightened that he might not be as indifferent to Bianca as he was trying to pretend. It was disturbing to discover how much her body ached at that thought.

*   *   *

Her two days in London passed in a whirl of activity. She did visit a hairdressers, but only to learn how to dress her long hair in several more sophisticated styles. It was far too attractive and healthy to cut, the stylist told her firmly, and Emma was relieved.

At first she had felt uncomfortable spending Drake's money, but her new clothes were all part and parcel of the role she was to play he told her.

Even so, she spent carefully. Bianca would expect her to be worldly and sophisticated and she chose accordingly, half surprised herself to discover how easy it was to alter her appearance.

Drake didn't ask to see what she had bought and she didn't show him. On the second day of her stay he had arranged to have dinner with her at the hotel.

She was waiting for him in the cocktail bar when he arrived and frowned in astonishment over the large box he gave her.

'Get someone to take it up to your room for you.'

'What is it?' Emma questioned.

He smiled wryly at her. 'Something I suspect you'll have forgotten. Now, are you ready to eat.'

When he chose to be he was an entertaining companion. A little to her surprise, he didn't as she had expected him to do, scorn women's views and opinions as of being of no importance and they talked for some length on current issues, Emma finding it exhilarating to pit her wits and views against his. She was surprised when he glanced at his watch and commented that if they were to be ready in time for the Concorde flight in the morning they ought to be thinking of calling it a day. It was just gone ten, she realised, looking at her own watch, and as Drake left her just by the lift, and she watched his tall back disappearing in the direction of the foyer she wondered if he was really planning on an early night or if he had a date with someone else . . .

She still smarted from his remark that he could look at and touch her body if he wanted to, the more so because she knew irresistibly that it was true. She wanted him to make love to her; and that was half the reason she found his company so exhilarating. Tonight listening to him talk at one point she had glanced at his hands and had immediately pictured them touching her skin. As she got in the lift she shuddered slightly. She had to stop thinking of him in that context. For them to become lovers would do nothing but complicate the situation still further. She didn't love him, she reminded herself, she simply wanted him physically.

As she got out of the lift and unlocked the door to her room it struck her rather ironically that she had come a long way from the woman who had considered herself so immune to physical desire— and in a very short space of time.

She had forgotten the box Drake had given her until she saw it lying on the bed. Curiously she undid the wrapping, glancing at the name written on it. It wasn't one she recognised but to judge from the quality of the box, it belonged to an expensive and exclusive establishment.

At first the layers of tissue paper obscured its contents from her view but as she moved them her hand stilled, her heart racing painfully.

Drake had bought her underwear; expensive, exclusive underwear, all of a highly sophisticated design—underwear such as the women in his life must wear, she decided, studying the beautiful detail on a cream satin bra. In all there were half a dozen sets of underwear; all expensive and understated; not bridal as Camilla's had been, or deliberately provocative, and yet somehow because of their very sophistication and the fact that he had chosen them, acutely but subtly sexy.

She wanted to send them back to him, but common sense warned her not to. She wouldn't put it past him to find some highly embarrassing and pointed way of ensuring that they were returned, and besides he was right; she *had* forgotten about underwear, and if Bianca was half as formidable as he had intimated she would pounce on and use to her own advantage any hint at all that they were not really engaged.

Although she tried hard not to show it, Emma was extremely excited about the thought of her Concorde flight. Normally such a luxury would have been completely out of her reach, but now Drake, albeit for reasons of his own, was making it possible for her, and she was determined to enjoy it.

Enjoy it she did, at least until she caught Drake eyeing her with an amused and comprehending smile. When she saw it she tried to feign cool indifference, turning away from him, angry with herself for appearing so gauche.

His hand covered hers as they lay folded in her lap, the firm squeeze he gave them making her turn her head quickly to look at him.

'I wasn't laughing at you,' he drawled; as always, infuriating her with his astuteness. 'It's extremely refreshing to see someone genuinely enjoying something. You're as prickly as a little hedgehog aren't you . . . I can see we're going to have some fireworks ahead of us . . . especially if you keep on glaring at me like that,' he added in a soft murmur. 'Remember we're supposed to be in love.'

'*We're* supposed to be,' Emma asked cynically, 'or I am.'

He studied her for a moment. 'Women generally show their feelings more openly than men, but I promise you while we're staying in New York you needn't have any worries about me fulfilling my role Emma. Just see that you fulfil yours.'

The flight was uneventful; their arrival in New York smooth and well organised, and not for the world would Emma have wanted Drake to see as they drove out of the city in their hire car, just how nervous and tense she was. However, as always, his ability to read her thoughts and see into her mind made any subterfuge on her part a mockery.

'Stop worrying,' he told her laconically, negotiating the busy freeway traffic with an ease that Emma could only envy. 'I'm the one who should be doing that.'

'What will you do if Giles won't buy the magazine?' she asked, wondering for the first time what would happen in that event.

'Run it down,' he responded crisply, 'although I'm loath to do that because it will mean people losing their jobs. From a personal point of view it isn't an asset that particularly appeals. I wanted the parent company because it fits in nicely with the rest of my organisation, but I don't have the time or the inclination to work on the magazine to build it up to what it should be. Contrary to what you seem to think owning a girlie magazine does absolutely nothing for me Emma,' he added drawlingly. 'I much prefer the real thing.'

'Yes, I'm sure you do.' Emma flicked him a disparaging glance as she studied the busy traffic. During their flight out she had done some careful thinking. She was vulnerable to him sexually and they both knew that, but she would be a fool to allow that vulnerability to undermine her to the extent that she became physically involved with him. He could have virtually any woman he wanted; if he did make love to her, it would simply be on the impulse of the moment, and she was beginning to have the uneasy suspicion that apart from severely damaging her pride and self-respect to be simply another casual affair in his life would not be enough.

At this stage she wasn't prepared to take her line of reasoning any further. It was enough that she had seen the warning light flashing.

The Fords' home was in New York State, imposing and extremely gracious. They had had to announce themselves to the guard on the gate before they were admitted; and the long drive, that eventually swept round to end in a small circle adjacent to a porticoed entrance was certainly impressive. Even so, Emma did not think she would care to live in such splendid isolation, so cut off from the world, guarded against it.

A manservant opened the door for them, nodding a grave recognition to Drake.

'Drake darling . . .'

The hard tip-tap of high heels along a tiled floor alerted Emma to her presence long before their hostess stepped into the ornate black and white tiled hallway.

Blonde and tall, she was so immaculately groomed and made up that she looked almost unreal Emma thought wonderingly, suddenly conscious of her own creased skirt, and no doubt tacky make-up. No wonder Drake had insisted on that hurried shopping spree. This woman looked as though she spent a fortune on her face and figure. Older than she was herself, Emma guessed; she was nonetheless extremely beautiful; almost impossibly so, every blonde hair in place, her silk dress clinging to her model-thin figure.

Her heavy, oriental perfume embraced Emma at the same time as its wearer embraced Drake.

There was no mistaking the sensuous way in which she draped herself along his body, carmine finger nails pressing into the thick darkness of his hair, her mouth raised for his kiss.

'Oh come along darling,' Emma heard her purr. 'I'm sure your little fiancée won't mind you kissing me.'

Emma took note of the derogatory 'little', and said coolly, surprising herself, 'On the contrary, I should mind very much indeed.'

It didn't take much acting to let her eyes shoot cold sparks in Bianca's direction, nor to move closer to Drake, her fingers gripping his arm so that he could not return Bianca's embrace.

For a moment Emma could not define the expression in his eyes as he looked at her and then she realised it was surprise. So she had surprised him for once had she? She was just beginning to recover from the shock of her own behaviour and realise what a ridiculous picture they must present, the two of them clinging like limpets to the one man, when she heard other footsteps, more measured and heavy than Bianca's, coming down the hallway towards them. Bianca released Drake immediately, but not before she had flashed Emma a challenging, glittering glare.

'Ah, there you are darling,' Emma heard her saying gaily. 'Our guests have arrived.'

The man who came to greet them was in his late fifties. Tall, with a shock of white hair, he must once have been handsome and still retained that powerful aura of attraction many older men possessed. He smiled warmly at both Emma and Drake, shaking Drake's hand and studying Emma with warm eyes.

'Well you've really surprised me this time Drake,' he said at last. 'When Bianca said you were bringing your fiancée with you, I must admit I was surprised, but now that I've seen her I can only applaud your choice. You're a very lucky man.'

'I think so.' Drake's smile caressed her flushing skin, his fingers interlinking with hers, as he raised them to his lips and then slowly kissed each one. Emma was totally flabbergasted. She wanted to snatch her hand away, but the sensation of his mouth against her skin was too blissful to resist. As always when he touched her the power of her response to him was unnerving. She wanted to melt into him, to touch his hair, his skin, to lose herself completely in him.

'Anyone can tell you're only very newly engaged,' she heard Giles laughing. 'It's a long time since Bianca looked at me the way Emma's looking at you Drake. I envy you old man.'

Emma was so scarlet she felt her skin was

burning off her bones. How could she have been so stupid. She dared not look at Drake. However, Bianca created a diversion, her voice shrill and bitter as she said icily, 'But then you're not Drake are you, darling?'

There was a small, unpleasant silence, which Drake filled by saying calmly, 'I wonder if we could go to our rooms. Very unsociable of us I know, but it's been a hectic day.'

'Of course you can.' Giles was instantly the concerned host. 'I'll get Bates to take up your bags. Why don't you both rest until dinner time. You're here for a fortnight, so we've plenty of time to discuss business.'

The room Emma was shown to was magnificent. Overpoweringly so, and she detected the hand of a professional interior designer in the mixture of fabrics and colours. She had her own bathroom; and a walk-in wardrobe room, far too large for the clothes she had brought with her. So this was how the very rich lived, well she didn't envy them ... Despite Giles' money there seemed precious little harmony or happiness in this house. She had seen the way his mouth tightened and his eyes grew bitter when Bianca made her acid statement. She herself had had no need to act; she had been too startled by the other woman's comment to hide her surprise. What made it even more surprising was that she should say it in front of the woman her ex-lover was going to marry. Drake had been right; she was a very very formidable woman—and an extremely dangerous one Emma suspected. Dear God if she were genuinely engaged to Drake and in love with him she doubted if she would have stood a chance. At least she was free from the burden of emotional involvement with him and therefore immune to most of Bianca's poisonous darts.

She glanced at her cases, thought about unpacking and then remembered that the house was staffed. Better to start off by giving Bianca as little ammunition as she could. She wasn't going to allow the other woman to make her feel gauche or unsophisticated and if no one came to unpack for her she could always do it herself later.

Dinner tonight would be an extremely tense affair she suspected, wondering what to wear. If she was too dressed up she would feel uncomfortable and embarrassed, and yet she didn't want to let Drake down by not dressing as his fiancée would be expected to.

Another door in the wall behind the bed caught her eye, and she glanced at it. There was a key in it on her side, and she walked over to it, trying the door. It was unlocked. She wondered if she and Drake had been given connecting rooms. It seemed highly likely, not that she needed to worry about that. She had the key, and Drake would be far too busy keeping Bianca at bay to have any time to spare for her.

Perhaps she ought to ask for his advice about dinner, and she had better do it now, she decided, just in case he was going to have a rest. Knocking briefly she turned the handle and walked through. The room was very similar to her own, and Drake was over by the window, staring out of it, hands in the pockets of his pants, his jacket lying discarded on a chair.

'Drake?' He turned round as he heard her, and she saw that he was frowning. 'I was just

wondering about tonight,' she told him. He had
removed his tie, and unfastened several of his shirt
buttons. She could see the dark tangle of hair
shadowing his chest and her own seemed to
tighten suddenly, strangling her voice. 'I'm not
sure what I ought to wear . . . I don't want to don
my full formal regalia, if . . .'

'Umm . . .' His frown deepened suddenly and he
lifted his head staring towards the door on to the
landing. In half a dozen lithe strides he had
crossed the distance that separated them, and as
Emma protested heatedly he pulled her into his
arms, his fingers locking in her hair and holding
her mouth a prisoner beneath his as he kissed her
deeply and almost roughly.

Robbed of breath, Emma struggled to fight free,
furious with him for his behaviour. His free arm
clamped her against his body and she could feel
the deep thud of his heart against her; the steely
strength of his thighs.

A weak tide of need poured through her,
destroying her resistance. She made a sound beneath
his mouth, half protest, half plea and then her arms
were round his neck, her body melting into his. She
wasn't aware of the approaching footsteps, only of
Drake's hand moving from her back to her breast,
exploring its firm contours. A tug and her silk shirt
came free of her skirt. Drake's palm felt warm
against her midriff. She was overwhelmed by a need
to feel his skin against hers and she trembled wildly,
drowning beneath his kiss.

'Good heavens! Drake darling I need to see you
alone for a few minutes. Perhaps your little
fiancée . . .'

Bianca's voice chilled the heat in Emma's blood.

She tensed automatically, but Drake didn't release her, merely lifting his mouth from hers to turn his head and say in a softly slurred voice. 'Not now Bianca . . . can't you see that I'm busy . . .'

Emma looked at the other woman wondering at her hardiness. In her shoes, she suspected that she would have crawled out of the room if Drake had spoken to her like that, but instead Bianca merely smiled tightly and raised thin eyebrows to say sweetly, 'Darling you *have* changed . . . Since when has sex been more important to you than business?'

Emma didn't have to fake the tide of angry colour sweeping over her skin. Bianca really was a first-class bitch she thought, stunned by the other woman's persistence.

'Sex might not be,' Drake returned in an even drawl, 'but love certainly is.'

'Love?' At last Emma saw Bianca change colour, her eyes wild with rage as she glared from Emma to Drake. 'Are you trying to tell me that you love her, Drake?'

'I'm not *trying* to tell you anything,' he said calmly. 'I'm simply stating a fact. And now if we could please have a little privacy. I was very dubious about staying here,' he added coolly, 'in fact I think it might be an idea if we left and booked into an hotel, although of course Giles will want to know why.'

With another furious glare at Emma, Bianca opened the door. 'You might think you can deceive me, Drake,' she said softly, 'but you can't. I don't know what game you're playing, but you're not as indifferent to me as you're pretending, and before you leave here I'll prove that to you *and* your little fiancée.'

CHAPTER SIX

EMMA sat through dinner in a haze, feeling more like someone observing the behaviour of actors involved in a TV play rather than a supposed participant in what was going on.

If she hadn't still been tussling with the effects of Drake's ability to arouse a hitherto unknown sexual hunger deep inside her she might have been able to be almost amused by Bianca's behaviour. The woman was pure bitch, Emma reflected without malice. The fact that her husband was watching and listening to her attempts to draw Drake's attention to herself and keep it there, appeared to concern her not in the least. Towards Emma when she did have occasion to speak to her, her manner was both off-hand and distinctly contemptuous.

Once or twice Emma thought she saw a look in Giles's eyes which indicated that he was not quite as besotted by his wife as she seemed to think, and it occurred to Emma that Bianca suffered from a dangerous degree of over-confidence. In many ways she reminded her of Camilla and her blood ran chilly to think that her young sister could, in time, turn into another Bianca.

When dinner was over, and Emma noted that for differing reasons neither she nor Bianca had done justice to the excellent food, Giles suggested that they all retire to the drawing room.

'No business talk tonight,' he said with a smile,

to Drake. 'I believe in fair play, and as I know to my cost transatlantic flight is particularly draining.'

'But darling.' Bianca's voice dripped venom as she poured the coffee. 'You forget how much younger than you Drake is.'

There was a moment's awkward silence and then Drake interposed smoothly, 'Younger maybe, but I quite agree. Besides,' he glanced at Emma, and her cheeks caught slow fire from the sexual appreciation of his look, 'there are other reasons why I'd appreciate an early night . . .'

Emma had no need to fake her blush or her confusion. Bianca's laugh seemed particularly high and false. 'Good heavens Drake,' she said shrilly, 'where on earth did you find her, she's positively Victorian!'

'Ignore Bianca, my dear,' Giles counselled Emma in a kind voice. 'Like a good many men with something of a reputation where women are concerned, when it comes to his own woman, Drake appreciates rarity value.'

While half of her was inclined to object to the blatant derision of his remark, Emma couldn't help responding to the pain in her host's eyes as they rested on his wife's tautly bitter face. 'I'm afraid Bianca has grown too used to being the centre of male attention to appreciate the company of another woman, especially one as attractive and feminine as yourself. Drake is known as a shrewd businessman, and I can see he's been equally shrewd in his choice of future wife.'

Bianca who had caught the last part of her husband's comment said bitchily, 'Oh I quite agree, Giles. What is it they say? If a man wants to be securely married he should choose a plain wife.'

Had she in reality been engaged to Drake, there was just enough truth in that comment to cause real pain, Emma thought wryly. She knew quite well that she was no true beauty; certainly not as she suspected Bianca judged her own sex, and she only had to think of the beautiful women Drake had escorted publicly over the last twelve months to admit that she herself was way, way out of their league, but she was not engaged to Drake; she was not emotionally involved with him, therefore she was completely safe from Bianca's vitriolic comments. So why this feeling of acute pain; why this need to glance uncertainly at Drake as though needing his support and reassurance?

Confused by her own reactions Emma was unaware of Drake moving until she felt the hard reality of his arm round her waist, her body responding irresistibly to the warmth and security of his—so irresistibly that her breath caught in her throat, her eyes focusing blindly on his face as she tried to come to terms with the emotions rioting inside her. You should have been an actress my girl, she told herself hardily, you certainly have a gift of throwing yourself wholeheartedly into your part.

'Emma has a beauty of spirit and personality which has far more appeal than anything manufactured by cosmetic surgeons and beauticians,' Drake responded calmly.

His defence of her was everything that, as his fiancée, she could have wished for. From the look on Bianca's face it was plain that the older woman was furious, and Emma wondered about Drake's remark. Bianca's features were so perfect that they could owe more to a good plastic surgeon than to nature, and for the first time she felt something akin to pity for the older woman. She had a loving husband; everything that his wealth could buy and still she wasn't happy. Nor ever would be Emma thought intuitively, even if that husband was Drake; Bianca would always want what just lay over the next hill ... the next man. Almost as though she sensed her pity the older woman glared at her, and Emma knew that she had made an enemy; not just because she was Drake's 'fiancée', but in her own right.

Shortly after that they said their good nights. Emma wasn't sorry to be leaving the drawing-room, which for all its elegance and expensive furnishings was a cold, unwelcoming room.

As she hesitated outside her bedroom door, Drake's hand on her wrist stopped her from opening it, and she allowed herself to be guided in the direction of his own door. Once inside he closed it behind them, and as he turned she saw that he was frowning; the strain of the evening plainly showing in his face.

'Thanks for your support downstairs,' he said, tossing the words casually to her over his shoulder as he discarded his evening jacket. 'God what a bitch that woman is, she was determined to create as much havoc as she possibly could.'

'Yes, I think if we were really engaged, we'd be in the middle of an extremely destructive row right now,' Emma agreed tiredly, remembering some of Bianca's bitchy remarks about Drake's previous womenfriends. Every remark she had made to Emma had been carefully designed to undermine her self-confidence, to throw in her face the fact that Drake was an extremely desirable and highly sexual man—as if she didn't already know.

'A row?' Emma could see Drake through the dresser mirror. The fine silk of his white shirt emphasised the muscular lines of his body. Of its own volition her body responded to its masculinity, her pulse rate increasing fractionally, the muscles in the pit of her stomach tightening. It really was amazing; the logical side of her nature retained enough control to tell her how illogical it was that she should respond so quickly and so intensely to a man who, on the face of it, was everything she most detested. Oh the perversity of human nature. Thank goodness, this was all simply a charade, and that she had the good sense to see exactly what sort of man lay behind the smooth urbanity with which he had countered Bianca's attacks on her tonight.

'Umm, Bianca is proving even more troublesome than I had envisaged.'

'Perhaps she does genuinely love you.'

It was a comment she had not intended to make and from the frown scoring between Drake's eyebrows it was not one he had expected to hear. 'Love?' His eyebrows straightened and lifted. 'My dear Emma, don't be naïve, that woman doesn't love anyone other than herself . . .'

The contempt he felt towards Bianca was quite plain to hear, and Emma echoed his frown although for different reasons. 'Are you always so contemptuous of the women you sleep with?'

For a moment Drake checked, and then he answered in a laconic drawl, 'If they merit it, then yes.'

'A psychiatrist might be curious to know why

you choose women you can only despise to share your life.'

'Meaning that I must be inadequate in some way?' And before she had a chance to reply, he answered his own question. 'Not necessarily so. I suspect the majority of men are looking for a woman who combines perfect features and figure with a perfect nature. It can hardly be held to be our fault that Mother Nature rarely sees fit to wrap all three in the one package.'

His cool mockery and taunting dismissal of her sex stung Emma into retorting, 'If men weren't always so keen to debase and exploit physical beauty in women perhaps they might . . .' She broke off angrily when she heard Drake's soft laughter.

'If Bianca could see you now she wouldn't be in such a hurry to dismiss you as a nonentity. There's an awful lot of passion lurking beneath that cool surface, isn't there?'

'I'm a normal, intelligent human being,' Emma responded, calming down a little, 'and like other intelligent human beings, I'm capable of having strong feelings on a variety of subjects.'

'So I've noticed. What a pity one of those subjects can't be me, Emma mine, something tells me that you and I could be very good together.'

He had moved as he spoke and was now standing directly behind her. Emma could feel the heat of his body filling the small distance that separated them. She badly wanted to lean back against him and to feel his arms come round her, his hands caressing her body. The intensity of her desire shook her, forcing her to fight to banish it from her mind.

'Any involvement between us will only prejudice

your business discussions,' she managed to respond crisply.

'You think so? Very well. But we *will* be lovers, you and I, Emma,' he warned her softly, as he stepped away from her. 'Maybe not now, maybe not here in New York, but ultimately your body will surrender its secrets and its passion to mine, and you're a liar if you deny it.'

How calm, and dispassionate he was, Emma thought, listening to him. While her body shook and trembled at the visions conjured up by his words, he remained unmoved, but then how many women had heard those words, or ones like them from him before? His body was no stranger to desire, to wanting, unlike hers ... and yet she knew that in all honesty she could not deny what he had said; that some small masochistic part of her didn't even want to deny it. She didn't know what it was about her that made him want her; she wasn't like his other women. Perhaps that was it; perhaps it was the challenge she represented; the novelty value of her virginity.

She was trying to whip up inside herself a resentment against him but although her mind might revolt against his arrogant words, her body reacted to them as surely and undeniably as though it had been programmed to do so. Her body was her real enemy, not Drake, Emma acknowledged, because it was her body that would ultimately betray her with its craving to satisfy its need to be possessed by his. There was no logical explanation for what she felt; no learned or reasoned arguments that could be applied against a force so great that she literally shook with the intensity of it.

She moved towards the connecting door, knowing that he would not stop her.

'Leave the door unlocked,' he warned her as she opened it. 'We don't want Bianca leaping to any conclusions, and I wouldn't put it past her to have given the staff instructions to spy on us and report back to her.'

'Surely she must see that you don't want her?' Emma queried.

'Bianca is a woman who thinks her beauty entitles her to everything she wants from life. Facing the fact that that isn't so, means facing up to the fact that her beauty is not the powerful, invincible weapon she has always believed and that's something she'll fight strenuously against doing, because it's all she has.' There was no pity in his voice only contempt, and as though he read her mind, he quoted softly, 'Those who live by the sword, my dear Emma. Bianca has not cared who she has hurt in her greed and self-conceit; witness her attitude towards Giles tonight. Now she is a candidate for the shrink's couch,' he added referring to their earlier conversation, 'but don't under-estimate her, Emma. She's a very dangerous woman, in the way that a person who's obsessed can be.'

'Meaning she's obsessed with you?'

'Not specifically. What she's obsessed with is getting her own way; with proving to her own satisfaction that she has the power through her looks to compel men to give in to her, I just happen to be the man she wants at this particular moment in time.'

Initially inclined to dismiss his comments as callous; to brand him as an egotistical male far too

ready to see in Bianca an all too convenient Eve,
Emma was compelled to hesitate and re-assess her
own judgment. In many ways Drake was right and
in admitting this she was forced to concede that he
was a shrewd, almost intuitive, judge of character,
and that, combined with what he had said to her
about wanting her was sufficient to increase her
tension to the point where it was almost a physical
reality.

It would be hard enough simply to battle against
his desire to possess her, but she had to fight the
added hazard of her own feelings.

It was a long time after she had left Drake
before she managed to fall asleep. Her feelings
towards him were constantly changing; her
judgments almost hourly having to be amended.
He was so complex a character that fresh sides to
him were constantly being revealed to her. She was
like a child, fascinated by fire, Emma told herself
wryly, on the edge of sleep; she knew that contact
with it would hurt and yet, irresistibly, she was
drawn towards the bright glitter of its heat.

'Good heavens, what time is it?' Emma struggled
to sit up as a uniformed maid arrived with a tray
of coffee and biscuits, fearing that she had
overslept so badly that she had disrupted the
household.

'Just after eight,' was the smiled response.

In answer to Emma's anxious enquiries about
breakfast she was told that the two gentlemen
would be having theirs in the breakfast room at
nine o'clock, and that she could either join them or
have breakfast in bed, as her hostess was
apparently doing.

How the rich lived, Emma thought humorously, declining the latter. Now that she was awake, she was too keyed up to simply lie in bed. Would Bianca's behaviour prejudice Drake's hopes of selling the magazine to Giles?

The latter had seemed a shrewd man to Emma, but even the shrewdest of men could sometimes have their weak points and his was definitely Bianca. Emma had not missed the look of pain in his eyes at some of his wife's more contemptuous comments, and it didn't take a degree in human behaviour patterns to guess that like any other human being he would be more inclined to blame an outsider for his wife's indifference to him than to blame her. Emma had sensed that Giles respected Drake, and yet that respect must be tinged with some envy. Drake was a young man in the full power of his maleness, looking forward to life while Giles was looking back.

Showered and dressed Emma made her way downstairs, thanking the maid who gave her directions for the breakfast room.

Once a conservatory, it was massed with plants, its decor as carefully planned as that of the rest of the house. Drake and Giles were both there before her. Drake stood up as she walked in, the brief hard pressure of his hand on her arm and his mouth against her skin sending pulses of awareness jolting through her body.

There was a certain degree of tension in the air, Emma could feel it, and as she glanced questioningly at Drake, Giles greeted her, saying, 'It looks as though Drake and I won't be able to get down to any business today. My secretary is off sick, and I wanted notes taken of our discussions. I don't like using agency girls, and I positively loathe those infernal recording machines.'

He looked rather like a little boy, scowling ferociously as he admitted to this weakness. Although she hid it from him Emma was faintly amused that a man who was the head of a multi-million dollar empire couldn't bring himself to use a dictating machine. He was not alone; Emma had come across this phenomena before—and often from men who had insisted on computerising whole departments. Their excuses were normally almost childish.

Without pausing to think she offered impulsively, 'Could I stand in for your secretary? My shorthand speed is quite good, and . . .'

Before she could finish Drake had picked up on the suggestion. 'Great idea,' he approved, without giving Giles a chance to object. 'Emma my love, you're a real treasure. What would I do without you?'

After that the morning flew by so quickly, Emma could not believe it when the maid came in to tell them it was time for lunch.

Tactic, and counter-tactic, thrust and counter-thrust; as two skilled combatants in the same field Drake and Giles had put forward their differing viewpoints. As a fascinated observer, Emma could almost feel the point where the tide began to turn in Drake's favour, and Giles began to give ground slightly.

By lunch-time Drake had won his agreement to retain all the existing staff for a probationary period of six months, if they were able to conclude all their other negotiations satisfactorily and the business did eventually become his.

Emma had listened closely to everything that had been said and on a couple of occasions had been able to insert a deft comment of her own.

During lunch the business discussion continued, with Giles making one or two comments to Emma. At one point he turned to Drake and said admiringly, 'You've really picked a winner here Drake; beauty, brains and femininity.'

'The three graces,' Drake responded, smiling at Emma. When he smiled at her like that she had difficulty holding on to her commonsense. She was almost grateful to Bianca for the small explosion of sound she made, her expression derisive, as her mouth twisted in bitterness.

'Be careful darling,' she said acidly to Giles. 'Your little heroine might not be as sure of Drake as you think. She might be lining you up as a substitute. A role you should be used to playing by now. I'm going out,' she added, standing up abruptly. 'We're dining out with the Carltons tonight. It will be a rather formal occasion,' she added to Emma. 'I do hope you've brought something suitable with you. Unfortunately, I can't lend you anything, all my clothes would be much too small.'

Much too small? A size at most, Emma guessed, but she didn't say anything merely smiling politely. She wasn't here to get upset or offended, she was here simply to act as a form of protection for Drake, and personal feelings of her own weren't allowable.

'I must apologise for Bianca,' Giles murmured uncomfortably when she had gone. 'She's been going through a difficult time recently. The drugs she's taking for the depression she's been suffering from sometimes have an adverse effect on her. I suppose all beautiful women go through a similar thing as they get older.'

He was asking her to make allowances for his wife, and Emma smiled again, and said truthfully, 'I'm just sorry we're here at such a difficult time for you.'

'Don't let it put you off marriage,' Giles cautioned Drake on a lighter note.

'It doesn't.' The look he gave Emma literally made her toes curl and all her commonsense warnings to herself go up in sheets of flames. The man was as lethal as dynamite, she told herself. If it was possible to do such a thing he was making love to her just by simply looking at her. The sensation was an unnerving one.

After lunch the men continued to discuss business while Emma made careful notes. It was gone five before they finally called it a day, and she was stiff from so much unaccustomed sitting still. A long soak in a hot bath was definitely called for she decided as she made her way to her room. There was also the question of what to wear tonight. Out to dinner Bianca had said, and Emma preferred the elegance of being slightly under-dressed to going for over-kill.

After inspecting the contents of her wardrobe she decided on a simple silk jersey Jean Muir dress in a misty shade of lilac. At first she had been uncertain about the dress because of the colour of her hair, but the shade was one that did wonders for her Celtic skin and eyes, giving the latter a faintly purple depth that made them seem twice their normal size.

Having decided on her dress, she went into the

bathroom to run a bath. She doubted that they would go out much before eight, which gave her ample time to rest and then get ready. She had brought a couple of paperbacks with her and taking one with her she wandered through into her bathroom.

An expensive range of toiletries had been provided for her use but after uncapping and sniffing the bath oil Emma rejected it in favour of her own Chanel. The perfume reminded her too much of Bianca; it was heavy and sultry, and not to her own taste at all.

The bath was enormous and the water piping hot; the paperback she had bought on impulse a good choice. Time went by and Emma was lost in another world, lifting her eyes from her book occasionally to add more water and push away thoughts of guilt at her self-indulgence. At home there was never enough time for a long soak; or when there was Camilla was in the bathroom.

'Emma?'

She was so lost in her book that it was several seconds before she registered the sound of Drake's voice calling her name, and it was only when he called her name again, his voice closer this time, that she was galvanised into action, calling out breathlessly, 'Yes, I'm here Drake ... I...' Her voice was strangled in her throat as Drake pushed open the unclosed door. The towel she managed to snatch up was barely large enough to wrap round herself, her face pink with indignation as she glowered at him.

'Umm, Number 5.' His voice was light, amused almost, but there was nothing amused about the long slow tour his eyes took of her body still damp from her undignified scramble to get out of the bath, and very inadequately concealed by the small towel.

'You should have stayed outside,' Emma protested wrathfully. 'Why . . .?'

'*You* should have let me know before that you were in here. I called out at least three times, for all I knew you could have drowned in here.'

Giving him a scathing look Emma started to skirt round him. He was standing between her and the protection of her robe. He made no effort to help her, merely picking up the paperback where she had dropped it and glancing as though extremely interested in it, at the printed pages.

'Will you please go away and let me get dressed.' The words were gritted through Emma's teeth as embarrassment gave way to anger.

'What? And deny myself the alluring picture of my fiancée . . .?'

'I am not your fiancée.' Emma snapped the words at him, glaring at him angrily. 'This is simply a business arrangement—remember? And it does not entitle you to come walking unannounced into my bathroom.'

'Oh but I was announced——'

'Will you please go away.'

'What are you so frightened of Emma?' His voice was soft, dangerously so, his scrutiny thorough as he studied her thoughtfully. 'You're far more adequately covered now than you would be on a beach for instance.'

What he said was true; she wasn't frightened so much as far too aware of the contrast between his masculinity and her own femininity and her vulnerability towards him.

'You scared me,' she said at last, admitting only a portion of the truth, 'I had no idea you were there.'

'I came in to talk to you about tonight. There was something I forgot to mention before we left London, and Bianca's bitchy remarks at lunch reminded me.'

Emma longed to tell him that whatever it was could wait until she was dressed, but every feminine instinct she possessed warned her that to do so would be to concede him a very definite advantage.

She was standing within two feet of him, with her robe lying behind him on a chair, and he stood between her and the door. 'If you'll just give me a minute to put on my robe we can talk about it,' she suggested lightly, hoping he wouldn't guess at her tension. The smile that curved his mouth told her that he had, his eyes mocking her.

'I like you the way you are,' he told her smoothly. 'And I like it even more knowing that my liking it disturbs you Emma. Oh yes it does,' he said softly before she could deny it. 'When you're disturbed about anything your eyes turn almost violet. What worries you so much? Is it the fact that I might do this?'

There was no way she could evade his arms imprisoning her, holding her tensed body against the relaxed outline of his. He laughed softly deep in his throat when she glared at him. 'Relax tigress,' he commanded her as he bent towards her, 'I'm not going to hurt you.'

The moment he said the words Emma knew that he was lying to her. Oh, he wasn't going to hurt her physically right enough, but emotionally . . .

So intense was the sense of self-revelation she suffered that her body shuddered with the force of it. Somehow without her being aware of it she had become dangerously vulnerable to him; a vulnerability that could only spring from the deepest kind of emotional involvement and yet there was none between them. Her feelings for him were purely and simply physical; weren't they?

She was so deeply involved in her own thoughts that it took his fierce, 'Emma ... don't try and escape from me that way ... Look at me,' to focus her attention on the darkly tense expression in his eyes.

'Where were you then?' he demanded. 'Where were your thoughts?'

'On my sister,' Emma lied valiantly, 'I was ...'

'Forget her,' Drake advised her. 'Think only of this.'

The heat of his mouth searing hers shocked her body first into frozen immobility and then into fierce, heated life. As if governed by an inner force that could not be controlled by her brain, her hands lifted to his shoulders, seeking for and finding the firm curve of his nape and the thick hair that grew there. Her mouth parted at the insistence of his, not making any attempt to resist his sensual invasion, her body shuddered, alight with a fierce, deep hunger as his hand slid from her waist to her breast, cupping it through the softness of the towel, his thumb unerringly finding the burgeoning tautness of her nipple.

Aching waves of pleasure spread through her body, radiating outwards from his seductive caress. Unable to stop herself from shuddering deeply in response Emma closed her eyes. It was a mistake. Instantly she was transported to a world where the senses ruled. Behind her closed eyes images of Drake danced; his body supple and male, and completely nude.

Fire shimmered across her skin, the aching in the pit of her stomach intensifying. She was barely aware of the firm tug Drake gave her protective towel, knowing only that as it fell away and his hands moved over her back into the curve of her waist, holding her against him, she was consumed by a fierce need to have him go on touching her, holding her, caressing her, loving her. . .

It took her several seconds to react to what she had unwittingly betrayed to herself; seconds during which she drowned beneath the sexual expertise of his touch, intoxicated to the point of madness by the feel and smell of him, recovering only when her brain forced her to acknowledge the danger she was courting.

Why should she want his love? Sex was all he could offer her; and sex was all she wanted from him, wasn't it?

When she stopped returning his kiss Drake lifted his mouth from hers, brilliantly jade eyes studying the smoky, aroused grey of her own.

'Second thoughts? It's too late for them now Emma, and besides they'd be a complete waste of time. You want me,' he told her arrogantly, and it was the sureness in his voice, the male conceit adding victory to his eyes that gave her the courage to move slightly away from him, her body tense as she responded coolly, 'Yes, of course I do, Drake, but sexual wanting isn't enough I'm afraid at least not for me.'

She saw him frown and bent to retrieve her

towel, hoping he wouldn't notice the way her body reacted to his careless appraisal of it. When she stood up and re-secured it, he was still frowning and Emma knew she had to take what small advantage she had gained and use it against him before he guessed the truth.

'You surely don't suppose you're the first man I *have* wanted?' She managed to inject a small thread of amused mockery into the words and had the satisfaction of seeing his eyes harden, his mouth tightening slightly as he moved a step back from her. 'I'm twenty-six years old Drake,' she shrugged smoothly. 'Of course I've experienced physical desire before, but I made myself a promise years ago that I wouldn't succumb to it unless it was teamed with something else. You see,' she told him proudly, hoping he wouldn't challenge her; that he wouldn't guess that no man had ever aroused her to the fiery heights he had taken her to, 'I'm not prepared to settle for the second rate; for sex on its own.'

'You want "love" as well is that it?' he interrupted harshly, his mouth and tone openly derisive. 'People have wasted their lives looking for that elusive state,' he told her sardonically. 'What makes you think you'll be any more successful? You're so smug and secure locked away behind your own principles aren't you Emma? What do you expect me to do? Admire you for them? Well I don't find them admirable, I think they're the mark of a coward; a woman who won't allow herself to come down to earth and enjoy life as it is. There's nothing morally wrong about enjoying sex for sex's sake; rather the opposite. The love you dream of is an elusive, non-existent state of mind.'

Every word he was saying to her was driving the pain deeper into her heart. She had known right from the start what manner of man he was; it was pointless to cry aching tears inside now because she loved him and she knew that love would never be returned. 'What is it you want from me Emma?' he demanded explosively. 'What is it you want me to say? That I love you?' His mouth twisted. 'I thought better of you; I didn't think you were the kind of woman who demanded lip-service paying to a set of outmoded customs . . .'

'Stop it Drake.' The words came out huskily, betraying to herself her intense pain. 'Whatever you say to me won't make any difference. I want to give and to receive love; I want to share my body with a man for whom I feel more than just sexual desire.'

'*Just* sexual desire?' She could hardly bear the derision in his eyes. 'Oh Emma how you deceive yourself. Just ten minutes ago that same "mere sexual desire" had you going mad in my arms; hungry for my complete possession. Lie to yourself if you must,' he added curtly, 'but don't lie to me. Just remember when the ache of your body keeps you awake at night what you could have had and what you still can have, if you come and ask me nicely.'

'Never.' The denial exploded from her tense throat, earning a cynical grimace.

'You're chasing after rainbows Emma; looking for pots of gold that don't exist. You're the first woman I've ever met who I find as stimulating mentally as I do sexually. We could be very good together you and I, and the pity of it is that by the time you're ready to admit as much it will be way, way too late.'

'Meaning that you'll already have moved on to
the next woman; the next challenge,' Emma
retorted bitterly. 'I'm sorry Drake, but I want
more from a man than a few weeks' sexual
pleasure and then goodbye.'

'Well you know what they say.' His smile was
cruelly hard. 'Either you use it or you lose it.'

He was gone before she could add another
retort and childishly Emma followed him to the
connecting door locking it behind him although
she knew he would make no attempt to walk
through it. Drake wasn't that kind of man. He
didn't need to be, with women like Bianca around
she thought wryly, asking herself derisively if she
had locked the door not so much to keep Drake
out, but to keep herself in; to stop herself from
weakening and going to him.

It made no difference that she spent most of the
evening telling herself that she had made the right
decision. Every time she looked up from the meal
she was barely tasting to find Drake deep in
conversation with one or other of their fellow
female guests she was pierced with a jealousy so
acute that she could hardly contain it.

To make matters worse Bianca kept on
watching her; like a cat at a mousehole Emma
thought muzzily, aimlessly pushing a piece of steak
round her plate.

Giles's friends were a couple in their mid-forties,
the husband brash and too forceful for Emma's
taste, the woman relentlessly flirtatious, brittle in a
way that made Emma shudder inwardly and pray
that she herself never found herself trapped in a
life-style that necessitated such behaviour.

It was something she ought to take as a timely

warning, she told herself later on as they were driven back to the house. Marriage to Drake, if such a thing by some miracle were ever to come to pass would be a constant effort to be the woman Drake wanted her to be and she too would develop that fretful, anxious look, she had seen so clearly betrayed on Rita Vanguard's smoothly made up face. No, that wasn't for her. She wanted a mate she could share her life with; laugh with; love deeply and intensely. Which was one of the reasons she was still single, she reminded herself sardonically. Perhaps Drake was right, perhaps she was living in a fantasy world.

They were back at the house almost before she realised it, so deeply engrossed in her thoughts that it came as something of a shock to hear Bianca saying tauntingly, 'I think our love birds must have had a quarrel. Never mind my dear,' she said to Emma, 'they do say a double bed is a great place for making up and Drake was always at his best between the sheets or so I've heard.'

Bianca was playing a dangerous game Emma thought, chancing to see the deeply bitter look crossing Giles's face. She was playing with fire and if she wasn't careful she was going to get badly burned.

'Thanks for the testimonial.' Drake sounded laconically unconcerned by Bianca's remarks. 'Our apologies, if we've both been somewhat subdued this evening,' he apologised to Giles as they entered the house. 'Jet lag catching up on us, I suspect.'

'I know the feeling. Bianca should have been a little more thoughtful and given you a couple of days to recover before arranging anything. It always takes me at least forty-eight hours to get anything like back to normal.'

'Yes, but darling, you're at least thirty years older than Drake,' Bianca murmured sweetly as they walked into the house. Emma almost cringed for the other woman's unkindness. Although he fought hard not to show it, Giles had winced away from her cruel words. Drake's mouth was a hard line as he refused a nightcap, and as Emma turned towards the stairs he followed her, catching hold of her elbow to bend his head and murmur, 'Still believe in the magic potency of "love", after witnessing that little débâcle?'

'I doubt that Bianca ever loved Giles, as I conceive it,' she responded shortly, 'although it's obvious that he adores her.'

'And a relationship with love on one side and not on the other, isn't what you'd go for, I take it? It would be against all those high-minded principles of yours?'

'It would be a recipe for disaster,' Emma responded shortly, hating herself for the unruly thoughts he was arousing inside her; the insane desire to turn to him and tell him that she loved him; and that so long as he was a part of it, she could take any relationship he cared to offer her.

Was she completely mad, she asked herself as she paused outside her room. She had seen tonight, with her own eyes, the effect marriage to a sexually dynamic man could have on a woman. She personally might have found John Vanguard brash and insensitive to his wife's needs, but she had recognised instantly the powerful sexual aura he gave off, and it hadn't needed Drake's murmured remark that John had probably slept with every single woman at the dinner table apart from herself, to underline the man's sexuality. Drake had made the remark to torment her, but Emma had instantly looked at his wife, and had seen past the carefully lifted and made up forty-odd-year-old face and had seen the agony of the woman behind it; a woman still deeply in love with a husband who no longer fully had that love. Was that what she wanted for herself?

'Where do you go to when you get that look in your eyes? And don't tell me you're thinking about your sister again,' Drake demanded, roughly grasping her arm.

'I was thinking about John Vanguard,' Emma responded truthfully without thinking, gasping out loud in sharp pain as Drake's fingers hardened on her skin. 'Damn you,' he cursed violently. 'Just what in hell are you trying to do to me?' His voice was thick and unfamiliar, sending frissons of corresponding sensations curling down her spine. 'I've been going mad all evening with wanting you, aching so much that I can feel it in every bone; every muscle,' he ground out at her, 'and then you throw John Vanguard in my face as calmly as you please. I thought Bianca was the original bitch, but I'm beginning to revise my opinion. What were you wondering about just then? How good he is in bed? Why don't you ask Bianca?'

'Why not,' Emma agreed coolly, fighting against the flood of emotions his angry words had aroused. She badly wanted to tell him that he was mistaken but she daredn't. If she gave way now she would spend the night in his arms; in his bed, and tomorrow morning she would bitterly regret her folly. 'I'm sure she'd be only too glad to give me a blow by blow description; of your technique as well as his.'

The expletive that burst into the tense silence between them made Emma shrink. Used as she was to TV technicians' colourful language, this was something else. The fingers Drake had clamped round her arm tightened until they were bone white, a look in his eyes that made her regret to the depths of her soul her hasty words.

'Why bother getting the information second-hand.' His voice was a thick, angry grate against over-sensitised nerves. 'I'll give you a personal demonstration.'

The violence with which he thrust open her bedroom door was a shock to her already over-tense system. Panic flooded through her body at the anger she seemed to have built up inside him. Drake was no carefully controlled product of a middle class public school like most of the other men she knew. He had grown up in a rough, tough atmosphere and it had left its mark on him.

Instinct told her to take the course of least resistance and so she remained completely passive beneath the bruising pressure of a kiss designed to hurt and degrade. His teeth against her skin hurt and drew blood forcing an involuntary gasp of pain that gave him the leverage he had wanted, his mouth brutalising the soft sensitivity of hers.

'Fight me, damn you.' His voice was harsh and strange against her ear, her whole body trembling nervously with a mixture of tension and reaction. 'Show me that you're capable of some feelings at least . . . or is your lack of sexual experience merely a cover for the fact that you're completely incapable of feeling *anything*, Emma?'

It was so brutal that she had no way of shielding herself from the pain. She could feel the blood draining out of her body; the agony of having her own deepest most private fears revealed with all the brutality of newly formed skin being ripped away from a wound. The pity of it was that until she had met him she would not have been able to refute the taunt. It had taken him to show her the true depths of her own sexuality; to show her that she was indeed capable of feeling deep passion; intense sexual hunger and for a moment she was driven almost to the point where she wanted to abandon everything she had fought for and show him all the hungry need she felt. But she couldn't do that. Drake was an intelligent man, once his anger had cooled he would start to analyse her reactions and it wouldn't take him long to guess the truth. That was the one thing she could not bear. Always an intensely private person, Emma could not carry the double burden of loving him and knowing that he knew of that love and probably pitied her for it. Instinctively she searched for a means of self-defence and found it slotted away neatly in her mind.

'You said you wouldn't touch me again,' she reminded him huskily, 'you said you would wait until I came to you.' Slowly her confidence returned and she was able to look him in the face, knowing that all he felt for her was sexual desire and the look she could see in his eyes; almost savage in its intensity could only be sexual frustration.

For what seemed to be an endless span of time they simply looked at one another, and then Drake broke the tense silence to say rawly, 'Damn

you, Emma, for the cold-hearted, unfeeling bitch
you are.'

He was just on the point of turning away when
Bianca came up the stairs. Emma knew the older
woman must have seen the swollen bruised
contours of her lips because her glance lingered
glitteringly on them before she said tauntingly to
Drake, 'My goodness Drake what on earth have
you been doing to your little fiancée. She looks as
though she's been mauled by an animal.'

'Jealous, Bianca?'

It was a sign of just how much his control had
slipped that he should reply the way he had,
Emma thought, shivering a little as she saw the
look that passed between them; an intense, bitter
hunger on Bianca's part which she had no
difficulty in interpreting at all, and an angry
curtness on Drake's which was harder to understand.

She could appreciate that he could be suffering
from sexual frustration; after all wasn't she
herself? Hadn't she too experienced the sharp
claws of need his earlier caresses had unleashed
inside her; but Drake was an experienced man not
someone who had never known the full force of
sexual desire before and surely it took more than
the brief caresses they had shared to arouse him to
the point where frustrated desire had to be turned
into the sort of anger he was exhibiting?

'Why should I be?' Bianca had recovered some
of her poise, her red mouth curling into a taunting
smile. 'It's already obvious to me that your fiancée
can't satisfy you Drake. But I can.' Ignoring
Emma completely she moved closer to him placing
her hand on his wrist, smiling invitingly up to him.

Emma was completely stunned. It was the sort of behaviour one expected to read or to see on celluloid, but certainly not to experience in real life. Bianca was totally ignoring her, treating her as though she simply did not exist. Remembering the agreement she and Drake had made and her supposed role, Emma thought frantically, wondering how she ought to react. Easy, an inner voice mocked her, just follow your instincts and scratch her eyes out.

Effective, but hardly what Drake would want. She was Drake's fiancée at least as far as the rest of the world was concerned, and no matter what had passed between them privately, Drake had given her no indication that he wanted that to change; or that he might welcome Bianca's advances. When it came down to it, his business interests were of far more interest to Drake than any woman. Her mind made up, Emma acted. Placing her hand on his arm she moved closer towards him, noting that she had no need to fake the faint trembling that seemed to have invaded her, even to the extent of infecting her voice.

'Drake, what's going on? Why does . . .'

'I'll tell you what's going on,' Bianca shrilled back interrupting her. 'Drake's trying to fob me off by producing you. He's just using you because he doesn't want Giles to know the truth.'

It came so close to the mark that for a moment Emma was stupefied.

'You're becoming hysterical Bianca.' Drake had recovered his control, his voice cool and icily dismissive. 'The fact that you and I were briefly lovers long before you met Giles is no secret to Emma, and you're only storing up humiliation and pain for yourself by constantly trying to resurrect something that was never truly alive.'

'You wanted me.' If anything Bianca's voice was even shriller and Emma found it in herself to feel sorry for the other woman no matter how badly she was behaving.

'Did I?' Drake sounded bored. 'I seem to remember that the boot was somewhat on the other foot. You were the one who did all the running, Bianca,' he told her cruelly.

She went white and gasped out loud releasing his arm. 'You . . . you . . .'

'Bounder?' Drake supplied wryly for her. 'I never did pretend to be a gentleman, Bianca, and it seems to me that was what you liked about me as I remember it.'

'All right, marry her if you want to,' Bianca snapped back viciously. 'Take her to bed and make love to her, but if you think Giles will go ahead with that magazine deal when I tell him the truth, you've got another think coming.'

'If Giles had any sense the only action he'd take once you've revealed all to him would be in the direction of the divorce courts,' Drake responded. 'The only reason I've put up with your tricks, Bianca, is that I don't want to hurt Giles, but I've come to the end of my patience. Tell him what the hell you like.'

CHAPTER SEVEN

She had never in her life experienced so much tension as she was experiencing now, Emma thought wearily as she studied her face in her bedroom mirror.

The atmosphere in the house since Bianca's outburst three nights ago, had been virtually intolerable. The only positive thing to happen was that Drake and Giles were continuing to negotiate the sale of the magazine. Giles's secretary was now fully recovered and back at work, and having chatted to the older woman on several occasions, Emma had found her warm-hearted and intelligent. She also suspected that Marti was in love with Giles. Life was a constant series of almost macabre jokes, she reflected unhappily, and Drake was probably right, love was an impossible to reach nirvana; a hoax thought up by unkind and mocking Gods to torment lesser human beings.

Bianca was in a mega-sulk, which although in many ways easier to bear than her constant vitriolic outbursts made for a very uncomfortable atmosphere, but Bianca's behaviour wasn't the sole cause for her tension, Emma admitted to herself. There was also Drake; and her own awareness of him; her body's awareness of the fact that he slept in the next room; her imagination's cruelty in relaying to her night after night tormenting images of his body, powerful and sleek, capable of arousing her own to the very

heights of human experience. But in the trade off
to reach those heights she would be giving up so
much ... She would always have her memories, a
traitorous voice persuaded her; many women
married for friendship; for children; for calmer,
surer waters than those represented by Drake.

That way was not for her ... It was unfair and
weak. Better to spend her life completely alone ...
So why not take what was offered to her now; why
not allow herself the pleasure Drake could give her
and leave payment of the price for the future?

On and on the inner arguments raged exhausting
her mentally and physically, and Drake wasn't
helping. Every time he touched her or looked at
her, he turned the screw a little tighter, increasing
her hunger for him, wearing away her resistance.
Since that night outside her room he had had
himself completely under control. Which was more
than she could say for herself, Emma thought
ruefully. Today he and Giles had gone to see
Giles's lawyers and would be gone for most of the
day, which was probably why she felt so restless.

At last unable to endure the confining, stifling
atmosphere of the mansion any longer Emma
decided she would go into New York and do some
window shopping. She hadn't visited the city
stores once during her stay and it would be a way
of passing time.

Giles had said on several occasions that if she
wanted to go anywhere she had simply to tell
Barnes their major domo who would organise a
car for her, and without giving herself time to
change her mind Emma sought him out.

Although he expressed doubts as to the wisdom
of Emma going into the city centre alone, she

eventually overruled him, and an hour later was seated in the back of Giles's luxurious limousine travelling towards New York itself.

The sheer pace of life in the heart of New York was something that had to be seen to be believed Emma decided exploring the fashion floors of Macy's Department Store. American women possessed a panache and style that took Emma's breath away and yet she didn't envy them. Somehow in their search for perfection, of face, figure and lifestyle they had developed a hungry, almost desperate look of strain that made her wonder if at the end of the day the frenetic pace of life was really worthwhile. I must be getting old, she told herself ruefully looking round for a coffee bar where she could sit down and catch her breath. She hadn't bought anything; for one thing she had neglected to bring any money out with her, fully alive to the dangers of carrying cash in the city centre and neither did she have the credit card Drake had given her. She had hoped that getting away from the claustrophobic atmosphere of the mansion might bring her back down to earth; put her in touch with reality again, but all it had done was to emphasise the wide gap that lay between Drake and herself. Here in New York, as in any other international city, he would be completely at home, whereas she preferred the relative peace and simplicity of country life. Why was she bothering to convince herself of their incompatibility, she derided herself an hour later, stepping out into the heat and bustle of the New York streets; she was perfectly safe from Drake; he would not approach her again; the ball was now in her court; all she had to do was to withstand her own feelings.

Easier said than done Emma thought, blinking in the harsh sunlight. The sidewalk was crowded with people and she felt someone jostle her from behind, thrusting painfully into her side. She turned automatically to object, the sound strangled in her throat as she saw the man's raised fist, and realised too late what was happening. Fool, fool she chided herself mentally in the instant that it dawned on her that she was the victim of a mugger's attack. *Why* had she turned round, why hadn't she realised what was happening and simply let him snatch her bag; there was little enough in it. So many thoughts chased through her mind in the few seconds it took for the hard blow to knock her to the sidewalk that later she was to find it impossible to believe a greater time had not elapsed.

She was aware of pain exploding in her head, of her arm being wrenched excruciatingly, of noises all around her, slowly dying away as she became engulfed in a tide of unconsciousness, her last thought a panicky fear of simply being left here to die while all around her life went on. New Yorkers were notorious for their non-involvement in the violence that went on around them every day.

'Emma?'

The voice was familiar, but the anxiety in it wasn't, and Emma struggled painfully to analyse why the anxiety should be so perplexing.

'She's not speaking.'

There was something else joining the anxiety now, a harshness that was more familiar under-writing the masculinity of the voice. It was a voice that belonged to a man who knew what he wanted from life, and who took it regardless of any opposition. Oddly enough it was also a voice that reassured her; that made her feel safe and secure.

'Give her time. She's had a bad knock, there's bound to be an element of concussion. To be honest we'd prefer to keep her here for observation for twenty-four hours.'

There was a hint of disapproval in the other male voice which Emma now recognised as American, as though this had been a point of conflict at an earlier discussion. She badly wanted to say that she didn't want to be left behind; that she wanted to go with the first speaker wherever he wanted to take her.

'Emma?' She knew he had bent closer to the bed, because she could feel his breath fanning her skin. She forced her eyes to open and a sensation like a massive shock wave jolted through her system. She had never seen such darkly green eyes, was her first dazed thought, followed quickly by the knowledge that she *had* seen these particular eyes before.

'Emma . . . are you all right?'

There was that anxiety again and now that she could focus on him properly she could see it mirrored in his eyes; evident in the taut stretch of skin against facial bones.

She lifted her hand and was bemused for a second by the brilliant flash of light from the diamond on her engagement finger. Something in her expression must have given her away because he said thickly, 'It's mine,' and Emma had the distinct impression that what he was really saying was, '*You* are mine.' The thought made her feel secure and safe and she looked trustingly up at him.

'We're engaged?'

'Don't you remember?' He was watching her closely and Emma shook her head; she had several muzzy impressions of pain and then falling; and slightly dimmer ones of a huge house which for some reason she didn't want to return to. One thing was clear to her and that was that they were visitors to America, because neither of them had American accents, but why they were here she could not remember.

'What can you remember, Emma?' His voice was stronger now, firmer and yet still carrying an undertone of anxiety.

'Very little,' she told him truthfully. 'Just pain and then falling.'

'Temporary amnesia,' she heard the other voice interjecting curtly. 'That's one of the reasons we'd prefer her to stay here.'

Watching him frown, Emma felt panic well up inside her. 'Don't leave me here,' she begged, fighting back weak tears. 'Please . . .' His eyes narrowed as she reached out towards him, and she wanted to tell him that he was the only familiar thing there was; the only person who could provide reality in the strange empty world she suddenly seemed to have entered.

'I have no intention of leaving you, Emma mine.'

'Drake . . . I've just heard the news, how is she . . .' The man who burst into the room was vaguely familiar, older by far than her fiancé and yet still very attractive. The feeling she felt on seeing him was a strange one; a combination of liking and pity, but yet she couldn't understand the reason for those feelings.

'Still very groggy,' Drake responded. 'I don't want to leave her here alone and yet it's too soon to fly her back to England.'

'Good God you can't do that. No, she must come back to the house. We'll get a nurse . . .'

'No! No . . . I don't want anyone.' It was to Drake that she appealed, wanting to tell him that he was the only person she wanted; the only person she needed. The doctor was frowning again. 'This is all very irregular,' he began, but Emma over-ruled him. 'Please . . . I want to go with my fiancé.'

'Very well, but only on the understanding that you ring us if there should be the slightest change in her condition.' He was speaking to Drake not to her Emma realised. 'If she becomes sleepy or listless, we want to know about it. At the moment she's suffering slight concussion but if it should get worse.'

'What about her memory?'

'That will return once the effects of the blow and the anaesthetic wear off. She's bound to feel very muddled for at least forty-eight hours. You've been one very lucky young woman,' he told Emma severely.

'What happened?' Emma asked shakily, 'I remember falling. . .'

'You were mugged,' Drake answered curtly for her, 'but luckily for you a policeman saw what had happened and he brought you here. Again luckily, you had enough identification in your bag for the hospital to trace me.'

'And even more luckily, the gash in your head, although messy, was little more than a surface wound,' the doctor interrupted. 'We've stitched it

for you which is one of the reasons you're feeling
so groggy—after-effects of the anaesthetic. Some
people are more susceptible to it than others, but
you're also suffering a degree of concussion from
the blow. Didn't anyone warn you about the folly
of walking alone in New York?'

There were several formalities to be gone
through before the hospital would release her, but
at last Emma was free to accept Drake's help out
into the open air. The Mercedes limousine he took
her to was vaguely familiar. It belonged to their
host Drake explained when Emma checked
slightly. They were staying with an American
associate of his while he conducted some business
negotiations with him, he further told Emma once
they were all in the car.

'That's right,' Emma was told by the American
who joined them in the car and who Drake told
her was their host. 'We were in the middle of a
meeting with my lawyers when we got the news.
I've never seen Drake so uptight in all the time I've
known him.

Emma was instantly remorseful. 'Oh I'm so
sorry,' she apologised ... Drake was frowning,
and at first she thought it was because she had
upset his day, but his mind must have been on
other things because he simply shrugged and asked
her how she was feeling. In point of fact she was
feeling almost light-headed, and muzzy. It seemed
so strange to have lost part of her life. She knew
who she was; she knew she had a father and a
newly married sister, Drake was familiar to her
although she couldn't remember how they had met
or how long they had known one another, and yet
she knew that she loved him and that the thought

of being parted from him even for one night was almost unbearable.

She listened to Giles talking to her on the drive back to his house, telling her that there was no point in panicking and that her full memory would return in due course.

The house was vaguely familiar, which was reassuring, but the way in which Giles enquired as to his wife's whereabouts sent prickles of alarm racing down her spine, which she couldn't explain.

Drake had insisted on carrying her inside. To judge from the reaction of her senses to being in his arms, they could not have known one another long Emma judged hazily; such intense sexual excitement at merely being held against his body, feeling the steady beat of his heart did not suggest a long-standing relationship. She wanted to question him but felt too tired. Tomorrow they could talk, she thought sleepily as he opened a door and carried her over to a large double bed.

'Don't fight it,' he advised her, pulling back the cover and then tucking it round her. 'They gave you a shot to make you sleep. Best medicine in the world.'

As he tucked the cover round her, he turned to leave and Emma reached out to detain him, clutching his arm. The look in his eyes as he gazed down at her was one she found it hard to define. It was a combination of pain and a certain wry self-mockery she was at a loss to understand.

'Stay with me,' she pleaded, 'I feel so strange and disorientated . . .' She essayed a brief smile. 'Am I always this clingy . . .? Somehow it doesn't feel like me.'

'It isn't,' he assured her with a wry smile. 'In

fact you're almost infuriatingly independent, hence today's contretemps.' He disengaged her fingers and stood up.

Emma frowned. 'Don't I get a kiss?'

'Are you sure you really want one?'

It seemed a strange thing to say to her and Emma was puzzled by it. 'Is there any reason why I shouldn't?'

Before he could answer there was a brief tap on her door and Giles walked in. 'Sorry to interrupt but there's a transatlantic call for you Drake.'

'I'm coming now,' Drake responded. 'Try to sleep and I'll come up and see you later,' he told Emma, as he walked across to the door.

For some reason that comment worried her, but before she could discover why, sleep was washing over her in unavoidable waves, dragging her down into its warm darkness.

CHAPTER EIGHT

EMMA woke up dry-mouthed and tense, disturbed by a confused and somehow frightening dream, whose details she could not remember but which left her feeling unhappy and confused.

Her room was in darkness and she fumbled for a lamp switch, crying out in alarm as she knocked something off the bedside table. As she started to scramble out of bed a door was thrust open sending an oblong of light to illuminate the room.

'Emma, are you all right?'

She felt almost weak with relief at the sound of Drake's voice.

'Fine,' she assured him shakily, 'just a mild case of blind panic. I woke up and couldn't remember where on earth I was for a second.'

He came to the side of her bed and eyed her thoughtfully. 'And now you can?'

'Just about.' Her voice was rueful as she fought against the dizzying flood of awareness just having him standing close to her brought thundering through her veins. 'But that's as much as I *can* remember I'm afraid.' She looked up at him and frowned as she realised he was wearing a robe and that he must have been in bed. As she looked at the door he had opened she realised it must belong to an adjacent bedroom and her frown deepened.

'Something wrong?'

'Why are we sleeping in separate rooms?' The words were out before she could check them.

'Don't you know?'

His question threw her. Was it because their hostess, who she couldn't remember and who she had not yet seen since her return from the hospital, disapproved of couples sleeping together before they were married?

'Is it because Giles's wife would object?' she hazarded a guess.

'That's one reason.'

One reason? Emma shivered. Despite the warmth of the room and acting purely on primaeval instinct she said hesitantly, 'Drake please stay with me tonight. Giles's wife needn't know.' Her face flamed as he continued simply to look at her. 'What I mean is if she disapproves of the fact that we're sleeping together before we're married, you could be back in your own room by morning. I just don't want to be alone tonight.

'If I come into your bed, it won't be simply to sleep.' The blunt warning was reassuring. For a minute she had begun to wonder if they had quarrelled perhaps.

'I need you tonight,' she said simply, not knowing how else to convey to him how much she needed the security and comfort of his warmth beside her.

'Have we been lovers long?' she asked shyly as he slid off his robe and pushed back the covers.

'What makes you ask that?'

She had instinctively averted her eyes from the satin gleam of his shoulders, caught off guard by the tight spiral of excitement building up inside her; an excitement that was spiked with something approaching fear, an emotion akin to the sensation she had experienced as a child when doing something she knew she ought not to do. Quite ridiculous really. She reached out to switch off the lamp and the light from it fractured against the diamond of her engagement ring.

'Leave it on.' Drake's voice was rough, sending prickles of alien sensation across her tender nerve endings. 'I want to see you when I make love to you, and no, we haven't been lovers long, why do you ask?'

He was watching her so closely Emma felt sure he must be able to penetrate the protection of the bed-clothes and see the wave of colour washing up over her body.

'It's simply the way I react to you,' she replied helplessly, unable to fabricate a lie.

'Meaning?'

He was lying on his side, his head propped up on one hand, the soft glow of the lamp emphasising the tanned healthiness of his skin. She wanted to reach out and touch him but she felt too shy, inhibited almost. It must be something to do with her amnesia Emma thought uncertainly.

'Meaning,' he prompted again.

Groping to find a lucid explanation for sensations and emotions she could only half grasp herself Emma said hesitantly, 'It's just that I find you so . . . so sexually overwhelming,' she told him honestly, 'almost shatteringly so. It unnerves me,' she admitted. 'It seems as though such a reaction is alien to my personality.'

'In many ways it is. You're a very private, independent person Emma, and I suspect that part of you deeply resents finding me "sexually overwhelming".' When he quoted her own words there was a gleam in his eyes that made her skin

turn to goosebumps. She reached out to touch him
and then withdrew, puzzled by her own behaviour,
confused by the conflicting signals it was giving
her. One part of her said touch him, love him, the
other said don't, withdraw, hide. Perhaps it was
simply a side effect of her concussion and the
anaesthetic, bringing to the fore emotions she
normally kept hidden.

'Why are you looking at me like that?'

His question caught her off guard, and she
answered it honestly. 'Because I want to touch you
and yet part of me says I mustn't.'

'Ignore it.' His breath fanned her skin as he bent
over her, tracing the line of her jaw with tiny
teasing kisses. 'Ignore it Emma,' he muttered
hoarsely against her skin. 'Ignore it and make love
with me.' His lips found the delicate lobe of her
ear, his touch sending dizzying frissons of pleasure
spiralling under her skin. Her fingers were stroking
his body, exploring the hard maleness of his
shoulders, her senses urging her to abandon herself
to the rip-tide of pleasure surging over her. It
seemed impossible to believe that she had felt this
before; that she had touched him like this before
and that he had touched her and yet she could
remember nothing about it.

In some strange way it made her almost greedy
to absorb every sensation he aroused inside her, as
though she was motivated by some deep-seated
need to imprint them on her consciousness in a
way which could never be erased.

She was still wearing her underwear and the
gown they had given her in hospital—the same
clothes in which Drake had carried her upstairs to
bed on their return—and at the first touch of his

fingers against her skin as he untied the robe she
moaned with feverish pleasure, hungering for the
feel of his hands and mouth against her skin with
an urgency that assured her that whatever else she
had forgotten she had not been mistaken in
remembering how much she loved her fiancé.

As though in some way the small sounds of
pleasure and need she made deep in her throat
enticed and excited him Drake shuddered deeply
as he released the catch on her bra, pushing back
the duvet so that the lamp glow fell directly across
the aroused curves of her breasts revealing skin the
colour and sheen of mother of pearl tipped with
rose pink crests.

It was impossible and unnecessary not to arch
invitingly beneath the openly aroused caress of his
eyes, the sound of her name, thick and slurred as
though he had difficulty in enunciating it, causing
the muscles in her lower stomach to contract
achingly.

'Kiss me.'

Her mouth opened eagerly and hungrily beneath
the onslaught of his, spasms of pleasure rippling
through her body when his hands cupped her
breasts. She opened her eyes dizzily, feeling her own
sensual response to the sight of his tanned skin
against the paleness of her own. Like her he was
naked, and her pulses leapt and jolted erratically as
she looked down the length of their entwined bodies.
She ran her fingers lightly down his spine and felt
him respond, his teeth nipping the soft inner skin of
her mouth, the smothered sound of pleasure he
made as her hand moved from his spine to the hard
thrust of his hip all the incitement she needed to
shape the male firmness of his buttocks.

His reaction was instantaneous, his mouth leaving hers with a smothered sound of pleasure to ravish the tender curve of her throat, the light touch of his thumb brushing tormentingly across the aroused peak of her nipple an ache that could only be appeased by the moist dragging heat of his mouth and the erotic pressure of his teeth.

Emma cried out with pleasure arching feverishly beneath him, her nails raking the taut flesh of his back, her body on fire with desire for him. His tongue stroked her skin, teasing and tormenting; his hand splayed across the smooth skin of her stomach. She ached with an intensity that held her in thrall, and he was teasing her, Emma thought feverishly, her teeth closing protestingly on his skin and making him growl deep in his throat.

His hand moved lower, filling her with a sexual heat that burned through her veins like fire. Unable to stop herself Emma arched against him in supplication, gasping in aching pleasure when his hands grasped her hips lifting her and holding her against the aroused heat of his thighs. Without even being conscious of what she was doing Emma ground her hips rhythmically against him, crying out to him feverishly when his hands cupped her bottom and he moved thrustingly against her.

Above her his face looked dark and unfamiliar and a spasm of fear shot through her. Almost as though he sensed it, he stroked his tongue against her lips, teasing her with light kisses, slowing down the pace of their lovemaking, coaxing the wholly unexpected panic from her.

She reached out blindly to return his caresses, stroking him feverishly until he muttered her name thickly and moved against her in a way that commanded her response. The weight of his body against hers, the heat and pressure of his thighs, invoked a compulsion that couldn't be denied. Emma cried out in a mixture of pain and pleasure as he entered her; the pain unexpected but almost totally lost beneath the intensity of sensations his possession aroused.

He filled her body, taking it and making it a part of his own until she was mindless with the ache of pleasure he was arousing, urged on to some peak she could sense was there, but was unable to reach. She felt the spasms contracting his body and knew from the way he cried out her name that he had reached that peak without her. Disappointment shivered through her; disappointment and a feeling of self-reproach, but before she could question it she could feel herself sliding deep down into heavy layers of sleep massed like thick clouds, supporting and comforting her, dulling the unfamiliar ache and stilling the quivering shivers racking her exhausted body.

She woke up in the night comforted by the warmth and presence of Drake beside her, curling her body into his and snuggling up against him. She had thought that he was asleep but he murmured thickly, 'Keep on doing that and neither of us is going to get any sleep tonight.'

His voice brought her fully awake, a vivid sensation of self-disappointment sweeping over her as she remembered their lovemaking. She felt as though she had failed not only him but herself as well. She wanted to talk to Drake about it but something held her back.

'What's wrong?' He seemed to sense instinctively that she was restless although she hadn't moved.

'You tell me.' Her voice was faintly self-derisive but instantly he picked up on what was distressing her. His arms came round, curving her more intimately into his body.

'Emma, we ought to talk,' he began slowly. 'There's something . . .'

'Wrong with me?' she concluded for him bitterly. 'Do you think I don't realise that. I can't understand it.' Her body ached and she moved restlessly, ill at ease with herself. Were she and Drake experiencing sexual problems; had he concealed the truth from her? Could *that* be the reason they had separate rooms?

'Something wrong with you?' She thought he sounded faintly stunned but was at a loss to understand why. She could feel him tense against her and then suddenly the tension went as he said in a different tone. 'Ah yes . . . I think I understand. There's nothing wrong with you Emma,' he told her softly.

'Then why?'

'Shush . . .' The warmth of his mouth against hers silenced her protests his skilled hands soon coaxing her body to abandon itself completely to him. This time their lovemaking was slower paced, more sensual than urgent, her body responding to his caresses as indolently and instinctively as a flower opening to the sun.

'Still think there's "something wrong with you",' he teased with lazy amusement as she floated down from the stars he had taken her to.

She was too dazed and satiated with pleasure to respond, content simply to lie in his arms and let sleep claim her.

*   *   *

'How do you feel this morning?'

Drake was dressed; frowning slightly as he looked down at her. 'Okay,' Emma assured him.

'No signs of returning concussion. No further memory lapses.'

'None at all,' Emma responded, remembering with perfect clarity the pleasure of his body possessing hers. This morning she felt languorous and lazy, content to simply lie and doze like a satisfied cat. It was an effort simply to move.

'Stay in bed this morning,' Drake advised her. 'I'm going with Giles to see his lawyers. We should get everything tied up and then this afternoon . . .' he broke off as a uniformed maid walked into the room carrying a breakfast tray. 'See you later,' he told Emma, bending to kiss her cheek. 'We'll talk then.'

Talk? What about, Emma wondered curiously sensing that the words concealed some hidden emphasis. Although losing her memory was only a temporary thing it was intensely annoying, almost depressing in some ways. Still there was no need to panic. Drake could tell her all she wanted to know and they had been most definite at the hospital that her muzziness and confusion was unlikely to last more than forty-eight hours.

Too restless to sleep she got up and showered. The morning stretched emptily ahead of her. She missed Drake. This feeling of insecurity she was suffering from must be something to do with her concussion she mused as she did her make-up.

She saw the door opening in the mirror and her heart thudded violently with pleasure as she anticipated Drake's early return. But it wasn't Drake who walked into her room, it was a vaguely familiar woman.

'Well, well, no need to ask how *you* are this morning. Drake's a first-rate lover, isn't he?'

Bianca! Memory returned with a sickening thud as Emma recognised the other woman.

'It won't last though,' Bianca told her, 'Drake will use you for as long as it suits him and then he'll go on to the next woman. That's his way.' She glanced down at Emma's engagement ring and laughed tauntingly. 'Oh, I know all about that. Drake is using you to hide the truth from Giles. He doesn't want Giles to know that we were once lovers, and would be again if it wasn't for the fact that he's so desperate to conclude this deal. He might have deceived you, but he can't deceive me.' She laughed again. 'Drake would never involve himself with a woman like you for real, you're not his type.'

Emma felt the well of blackness opening up treacherously beneath her. She was dimly conscious of Bianca's face, its beauty marred by the two ugly patches of colour darkening her cheekbones, but then mercifully the blackness engulfed her and she was alone and safe.

'Emma?'

She recognised his voice instantly but refused to respond to it. What was the point? She had been awake when he walked into the room but had feigned sleep, buying time, wishing only that he would go and leave her alone with her humiliation. The first thing she had known when she came round from her faint was that Bianca had been telling the truth. She was *not* really engaged to Drake, but she had not admitted as much to the other woman. Frightened by her collapse, Bianca had sent for her housekeeper who had fussed and fussed until Emma was on the point of screaming. Desperate to be alone she had volunteered to go to bed and rest, but there had been precious little rest to be found. Instead her thoughts had gone round and round, trapping her in a mill-race of self-betrayal and contempt. Her memory had returned completely, but twenty-four hours too late.

Dear God, when she remembered how she had behaved last night. Even knowing that Drake was watching her she was unable to stop herself from shuddering with self-loathing. But Drake *had* known, she reminded herself bitterly, Drake had known and he had still . . .

'Hey, don't I get a kiss?'

His duplicity infuriated her. She wanted to lash out at him almost physically to make him ache with pain as she was aching, but in reality she felt forced to admit that she had no one to blame but herself. She had thrown herself at him and he, being the man that he was had simply taken what she had offered. It was as simple and basic as that. Now, despite the pain building inside her pride compelled her to find some means of protecting herself; of concealing from him how deep her feeling for him actually went.

'I hardly think so Drake.' She was proud of the crisp cool sound of her voice. 'I've regained my memory,' she added coolly. 'Unfortunately several hours too late.'

She was surprised by the dark colour burning along his cheekbones and by the anger she saw blazing in his eyes.

'I see. Hit you hard has it, the realisation that that moral code of yours wasn't quite as inviolate as you had believed. We're all of us only human Emma, you're no exception to that rule.'

'What are you trying to say? That I didn't know what I was doing?' She was torturing herself but was unable to stop doing it, unable to stop scorning herself for her own self-betrayal.

'Oh you knew what you were doing all right.' The mockery in Drake's voice made her skin burn. 'You were doing exactly what you've wanted to do ever since we met, however much you might want to deny it.'

'And I hate myself for it,' Emma told him bitterly, watching the way his face closed up and his eyes grew bitter, without understanding the reasons for them doing so.

CHAPTER NINE

USING a will-power and self-control she hadn't
known she possessed Emma managed to endure
the remainder of her stay in New York. She had
agreed to pose as Drake's fiancée for as long as it
took to conclude the negotiations safely, and she
was determined that she was not going to give
Bianca the satisfaction of seeing her run away.

Not that it was easy. They stayed on for a
further week while Drake and Giles wrapped up
all the final details, and during that week Emma
not only had to cope with the anguish of her love
for Drake, and the continual strain of hiding it
from him and pretending a curt indifference she
could never feel, but she also had to endure
Bianca's vicious verbal attacks which ranged from
outright statements that Drake could not possibly
love her to more subtle and sometimes more
painful innuendoes which luckily she managed to
totally ignore.

None of it was easy, but at last the final details
of the contract were agreed and both parties had
signed. Since she had confronted him with her
return of memory Drake had been controlled and
wary whenever they were together. Was he
frightened that she might demand the traditional
virgin's recompense for loss of her virginity? she
wondered acidly on one such occasion. But then
she reminded herself that he had known of her
inexperience, had *known* of it, and deliberately

ignored it simply to appease his own megalomania. That was what she found hardest to forgive; to understand; that he had known the truth but that he had quite callously ignored it.

On the few occasions he had attempted to bring the subject up; to talk to her about it, Emma had cut him off abruptly stating that it was not something she wished to discuss.

'What's wrong?' he had demanded on one such occasion. They had been deeply involved in the final details of the contract all morning and she had been able to see the exhaustion drawn into the fine-grained texture of his skin. Not only that but he was also distinctly tense and on edge, the mocking indolence she had grown to associate with him, displaced by a bitter wariness she could only assume sprang from her discovery of the truth before he had been able to exploit the situation to the full. When he had told her with such arrogant self-assurance that they would be lovers, she had not dreamed he would go to such lengths to fulfil his boast. And the pitiful thing was that it would not have been necessary. One smile; one false word of love and she doubted that she would have been able to resist him for much longer.

'What is it?' he had persisted. 'Disillusioned to discover that after all your body's capable of disobeying you and enjoying sex without love?'

It had hurt so much to hear him say the words. For one aching moment she had been tempted to tell him the truth, to blurt out that there might not have been love on his side, but there certainly had on hers, but she had restrained herself, telling herself that if nothing else she could retain some

degree of pride. He obviously didn't realise that
she loved him, and he never was going to realise,
she had told herself firmly.

'Is it?' She could still remember the way his
facial muscles had tensed as she spoke, almost as
though in anticipation of some mortal blow. 'We
obviously have vastly differing memories of what
happened,' she had continued blightingly. 'Enjoyment was certainly not the word I would have
used.' She had almost broken down then, but had
forced herself to remain cool and unmoving in the
face of his angry retort, closing her eyes to blot out
the sight of his tight, too pale face and glittering
eyes.

It was over now, she reminded herself, opening
her bedroom door. The contract was signed and
this evening they flew back to London. As far as
she was concerned she could not get home fast
enough. She was tired deep down in her bones; in
her very soul really. Tired and broken; aching with
the pain of her love and yet knowing there was no
surcease for it.

Even if they had not quarrelled, even if they
were still lovers the pain would still be there. She
didn't just want Drake's desire; she craved his
love; wanted and needed it so that it was a sickness
in her soul; a pain that absorbed all her energy and
will-power.

They scarcely spoke to one another on the long
flight back to Britain. Emma was glad. Her self-
control was at such a low ebb that she didn't
believe she could have said a word without
bursting into tears. It was only as they were
actually landing that Drake said tersely, 'Emma,
look we must talk, there's . . .'

'Nothing we have to say to one another really,' she responded quickly, not wanting to hear his protestations, his glib explanations of his behaviour. 'We made a bargain. I stuck to my side of it, and now it's over.'

'Meaning that *I* did not stick to mine?' he demanded bitterly.

Emma could not bring herself to look at him. Her mouth twisted slightly as she told him, 'In your own eyes I'm sure you did. After all you did warn me that you intended us to become lovers.' At last she managed to raise her eyes to his, using all the contempt and anger she felt at the sheer callousness of his behaviour to give her the courage to do so. 'It simply never occurred to me that you meant you would use any and every means at your disposal to do so. What's the matter Drake?' she asked mirthlessly. 'Are you so insecure; so uncertain of yourself as a man and a human being that you *have* to cheat?'

'You *wanted* me to make love to you.'

Now she couldn't look at him, and the hoarse tension of his voice made her stomach clench in bitter protest. The emotion he was projecting sounded so real, but she knew the truth.

'So I did. When I thought you were my fiancé; when I believed that we were in love.'

'You accuse me of deceiving others Emma,' he retorted brutally, 'but when it comes to deceiving yourself you're an expert. Do tell me,' he invited cuttingly, 'how was it you were able to persuade yourself so easily that you loved me enough to accept me as your fiancé; as your lover in fact?'

Another second and he would be guessing the truth Emma thought frantically, panicked into saying bitterly, 'I don't know. I only wish to God I did, because on a scale of nought to ten it rates a full one hundred as the worst experience of my life.'

After that he had said nothing, but she could tell from the angry white lines carved either side of his mouth that he was furious with her.

They went through Customs in a tense bitter silence, which was broken only when Drake commandeered them both a taxi.

It was already gone ten at night, but when he suggested that she stay at his apartment for the night Emma shook her head curtly, her scathing, 'No thanks,' drawing patches of dark colour to stain his cheekbones and add a curiously vulnerable appearance to his face, which somehow looked thinner, drawn almost.

He didn't try to argue with her, for which Emma was deeply thankful, but it was only when he had got out of the taxi that she finally felt able to breathe properly.

Knowing she would not be able to get rail connections all the way home at this hour, she decided to hang the expense and go all the way home by cab. She was just too weary to wrestle with the problem of finding cheap accommodation in London at this time of night and anyway she wanted the security and comfort of home; like a wounded animal she longed for the protection of the place she knew best, she thought tiredly closing her eyes and leaning back against the leather seat.

As she had expected when she got home the vicarage was in darkness. When he was not out, her father went to bed relatively early. She let herself in with her key, dumping her suitcase in the hall before making her way up to her own room.

It was so deeply familiar that she could scarcely believe how much had changed since she last saw it; first the realisation of her love for Drake; then trying to cope with it; to fight against his blatantly expressed desire for her, which had all been a complete waste of time, she reminded herself bitterly as she climbed into bed. Tomorrow she would have to start re-thinking the course of her life, but that was tomorrow, right now all she wanted was sleep and oblivion; and the longer it lasted the better.

The first problem she had not anticipated was her father's concern over her supposed 'broken engagement'. Over breakfast she told him simply that they had discovered that their personalities clashed, and while on the surface he had accepted this, she could sense him turning the matter over in his mind and carefully weighing it.

'You know you surprise me,' he told her at length. 'I should have thought your personalities would have meshed extremely well. Unlike Camilla, you need a man who can be strong enough to over-rule you on occasions. You don't respond to weakness Emma; probably because your own character is so unswerving.'

Emma tried to shrug nonchalantly. 'A broken engagement isn't the end of the world these days.' She put down her cup and faced her father. 'I was wondering if that post with David Carter was still open.'

Although he regarded her thoughtfully her father made no comment other than a calm, 'I think so. Would you like me to find out?'

'It might be an idea.'

'Running away Emma, that isn't like you.'

She could hardly tell her father that Drake was most unlikely to come looking for her with a view to persuading her that they were after all suited, so she took refuge in a brief shrug. She knew that if she told him the truth he would not stand in judgment, but talking about what had happened was still far too painful for her to discuss it with any third party. She never had been a person who found surcease in discussing her problems with others. No, all she could do was to keep herself so busy that there simply wasn't time to think or brood.

In the afternoon once she had unpacked she decided to walk through the village and up to the Manor. Sooner or later she would have to see Camilla. How was her sister settling down to married life, she wondered as she set out. She knew from her father that she and David had returned from their honeymoon the previous week, although her father had not yet seen Camilla.

Laura opened the door to her brief knock, beaming with pleasure when she saw her. 'Back from New York so soon?' Her eyes rested briefly on Emma's left hand, and swallowing the anguish burning in her throat Emma said lightly, 'Yes, it didn't work out as we hoped, so we decided to cut our trip short.'

Accepting Emma's philosophical attitude at face value she stood to one side to let her walk into the hall. 'Well these things happen,' she agreed. 'Have you come to see Camilla?'

Grateful for the fact that she hadn't asked any awkward questions, Emma nodded.

'She's in the sitting-room. I'll go and organise some coffee for you.'

Camilla was glancing through a magazine when Emma walked in. She threw it down the moment she saw her sister, and Emma's heart sank a little as she saw her petulant expression.

'You look marvellous,' she began placatingly, 'What a wonderful tan. I really envy you. How was Barbados?'

'Oh all right,' Camilla shrugged. 'Not as exciting as New York though I'll bet. Where's Drake?'

'I don't have the faintest idea.' Emma accompanied the cool words with a brief smile. 'The engagement is off.'

Camilla stared at her. She seemed about to say something, and then the door opened and David walked in. He went straight to his wife's side, kissing her warmly.

'God I never realised how dull estate work could be, or how distracting it is to have such a lovely wife.'

The adoration in his eyes as he looked at her sister made Emma's heart ache with jealousy. If only Drake felt that way about her. Something in her expression must have betrayed her because she heard Camilla saying with genuine concern. 'Emma are you all right, you've gone quite pale.'

'I'm fine,' she lied. In point of fact for a moment she had felt quite dizzy. It was an unnerving sensation making her remember the American doctor's warning about concussion. 'Jet lag I expect,' she added by way of explanation. 'I only got back late last night.'

'Emma's engagement's off,' Camilla remarked to her husband. 'What happened exactly?'

While David gently chided his wife for her brutality Emma made herself shrug and say as she had done to her father. 'Oh nothing very dramatic we simply discovered that we were poles apart in our outlook on life.'

'I could have told you that myself.' There was a certain degree of satisfaction in her sister's voice, and Emma remembered that Camilla had always liked to be the one in the limelight; and that she had always resented anyone up-staging her.

'So it's all over. What will you do now then?'

'I'm hoping to get a summer job working with Professor Carter.'

Camilla pulled a face. 'God how boring. No wonder you and Drake didn't suit. At least he knows how to have a good time.'

Emma was conscious of a sudden tension in the atmosphere. David glanced at his wife and frowned. Camilla's expression was tinged with a faint smugness and Emma felt herself tense in response to the heavy silence. Camilla always had enjoyed baiting David, and normally he was slow to respond, but this time she seemed to have succeeded. He looked very angry.

'I thought you didn't know the man all that well,' he said curtly.

'Oh no . . . well I don't,' Camilla agreed lamely, 'but one only has to read the newspapers. Oh do stop being such a jealous bore darling,' she chided him. 'Emma I'm afraid we're going to have to throw you out. We're going out to dinner with some friend's of Mama's this evening and we really ought to be getting ready.'

'There's plenty of time yet, Camilla,' David interrupted, still frowning. 'Emma is your sister and . . .'

'And I have to get back to the vicarage,' Emma broke in calmly. 'Enjoy your dinner party.'

As she walked home she wondered about her sister's marriage. Was Camilla growing bored already, or was it simply that she enjoyed making David jealous? And for so little reason. Her sister could be swimming in dangerous waters, Emma thought. She had rarely seen David look as angry as he had when she mentioned Drake's name. She wouldn't put it past her irresponsible sister to pretend that there had been more between herself and Drake than there had been simply to torment David.

Reminding herself that her sister's marriage was none of her affair Emma continued on her way home.

Over dinner she discovered that the post with Professor Carter was indeed still open; mainly because there were so few people qualified to fill it who were willing to work for the extremely small salary he was able to pay. She could live in at Cambridge, and the change of scene would do her good she told herself. There would be no memories of Drake there to torment her.

Several days later Emma reflected that she had forgotten that one took one's memories with one. It seemed impossible that she could have lost nearly half a stone in so short a time, but that was what had happened. When she looked in the mirror she barely recognised herself in the fine-drawn, almost haunted woman who stared back at her. The work itself was interesting; the pace of life in Cambridge with most of the graduates gone for the summer recess, drowsy and timeless, which probably accounted for her increasing restlessness,

Emma decided, trying to deny to herself that her restlessness sprang from the fact that she was missing Drake's dynamic presence.

She had telephoned Camilla on a couple of occasions but her sister had been abrupt almost to the point of rudeness to her which made it all the more surprising to arrive at her rooms one afternoon to find a message waiting for her saying that her sister wanted to speak to her urgently.

She got through to the Manor straight away. Laura answered the 'phone and, while she waited for her to find her sister Emma ran through all the possible reasons why Camilla wanted to speak to her.

'Emma?'

'Yes, it's me,' she confirmed. 'What's wrong?'

'It's David,' Camilla told her flatly, causing Emma's heart to drop. 'He's being so unreasonable.'

'What about?' Emma had long ago learned that there was little point in reasoning with Camilla until the full story was known. Camilla was not above enjoying a little self-dramatisation, and Emma waited patiently for the story to unfold.

She was not disappointed. 'He's got this crazy idea that I was involved with Drake. He's furious about it Emma,' Camilla continued when Emma didn't respond. 'He's practically accusing me of being unfaithful to him with Drake that time I was in London. Of course I've told him he's being ridiculous,' Camilla complained petulantly, 'but he just won't listen to me. You've got to help me.'

'By doing what?' Emma asked. 'If he won't listen to you why should he pay any attention to me?'

'He would if he thought you and Drake were back together again,' Camilla astounded her by saying.

For sheer selfishness her sister really took the biscuit Emma thought, too stunned to speak.

'Emma? Emma are you still there?' Camilla's voice sharpened with anxiety. 'Look Emma you've got to help me. It's really serious. I'm afraid that he might even divorce me . . .'

'Oh Camilla, don't be so ridiculous,' Emma started to say, but Camilla broke down in noisy sobs, interrupting her.

'You don't understand,' she wept. 'I think I could be pregnant, and we'd already planned that we wouldn't have a family just yet, David will probably start thinking the baby isn't even his, the way he's acting at the moment. I'm so miserable about the whole thing Emma . . . I've even thought of abortion.'

'No . . . no Camilla you mustn't do that.' There was genuine panic in her sister's voice and Emma remembered that Camilla had always had a deep-rooted fear of childbirth. Recently it had not been mentioned and Emma had thought she had got over it, but obviously she was wrong. Her sister was highly strung and emotional enough to cause problems for herself and the baby she carried, if she was not cosseted and cared for all through her pregnancy, and if David genuinely did believe that she had been involved with Drake . . . while her mind fought to grasp all the ramifications of what might happen, Camilla was still crying.

Fighting for self-control Emma spoke quietly, soothing her into mere sobs.

'You will help me won't you . . .? God Emma

I'm so scared.' She wasn't acting, Emma could hear the fear in her voice.

'What can I do? Do you want me to talk to David?'

'No . . . no that won't do any good.' Camilla was almost feverish in her anxiety. 'No Emma, the only thing that will work is for him to see you and Drake together.'

'But that's impossible,' Emma protested, her stomach muscles contracting painfully at the mere thought of seeing Drake again. 'Our engagement is over,' she reminded Camilla, 'I could hardly go to Drake and ask him to pretend that we're still together. Besides, David would never believe it . . . he knows that we've decided to go our separate ways.'

'You could make him believe it.' Camilla was on the edge of hysterics, Emma could feel it, and her own fingers tightened tensely round the receiver.

'Camilla, please . . .' she began placatingly, but her sister would not be soothed.

'You *won't* help me will you?' she sobbed angrily. 'You want David to divorce me. . . . You've always hated me . . . I. . .'

'Camilla, Camilla stop it, please,' Emma begged fighting against panic and the knowledge that she would have to give way. 'Try to relax . . .'

'How can I relax, when David is virtually on the point of demanding a divorce? Emma I'm so frightened . . .' It was a little girl wail and Emma responded automatically to it.

'All right Cam, I'll do what I can . . .'

'You'll get in touch with Drake and get him to come down here then?' Now that Emma had given way, Camilla was curiously practical. 'We're having a dinner party next week, if you could just bring him to that . . .'

'Oh Camilla . . . I . . . Surely David will guess the truth when he realises we aren't still engaged . . .'

'He won't know will he,' Camilla said impatiently. '*You're* working in Cambridge; Drake's in London, he'll just assume that you've made it up and . . .'

'And what? You can't preserve the fiction of our engagement for ever.'

'I won't need to. Once he's got over this ridiculous jealousy and I've told him about the baby, everything will be all right, I know it will. Oh Emma, I promise you I'll never ask for your help again if you just do this for me.'

What could she say? If it hadn't been for the fact that Camilla was pregnant she might have said no, but she couldn't rid herself of her fear that her impulsive, over-emotional sister might do something very silly if she turned her down.

'Very well,' she said quickly, 'I'll telephone Drake and ask him if he will come to this dinner party with me, but Camilla,' she cautioned her sister. 'You must remember that he could refuse.'

She rang him at his apartment that night. Although he was ex-directory he had given her his number during the days of their 'engagement' and for some reason she had kept it. 'For some reason', who was she kidding; she derided herself. She knew quite well why she had kept it; because it was a last link between them that she had not been able to bring herself to destroy.

He answered almost immediately, and it struck

her as she announced herself that he didn't sound in the least surprised; quite the opposite. It was almost as though he had been expecting her call. Sheer nerves, she told herself, fighting against an impulse to hang up. Her stomach was alive with nervous butterflies. Was he alone she wondered or was there someone with him ... Another woman...? Stop it, she warned herself, you're doing this for one reason and one reason only—to help Camilla.

'Emma ... how delightful to hear from you. What can I do for you?'

'I need your help,' she said baldly, cursing herself seconds later as she heard a sound that could have been a muffled curse. 'Emma, you're not trying to tell me that you're pregnant are you?'

Humiliation washed over her in a burning wave. She almost hung up there and then. 'No, I *am* not,' she retorted through gritted teeth, 'and if I were you would be the last person I...'

'Is that so? My goodness you have been busy since we came back to England haven't you?' he taunted. 'So if you're not ringing to break the news to me that I'm to become a parent, what do you want?'

He wasn't making it easy for her, but somehow Emma managed to outline the situation.

'And...?' he questioned smoothly when she had stumbled into silence,

'And I have promised Camilla I'd do what I could to help,' Emma told him at last. 'She's giving a dinner party next week and she feels that if you and I attended it together it would...'

'So you're ringing up to ask me out to dinner is that it? Emma, how delightfully modern of you.'

He was tormenting her deliberately, Emma knew that. Forcing down her panic and embarrassment she said curtly, 'I'm sure it isn't the first time you've received an invitation from a woman, Drake, so don't pretend it's so unusual.'

'Ah yes, but normally with an ulterior motive,' he responded softly. '*Is* that why you're telephoning me Emma? Because you want me to go to bed with you?'

Oh God, why was he doing this to her? She had a vivid and acutely agonising mental image of him as he had been that morning after they had made love. A surge of need and hunger swept through her body leaving her aching, shivering with the force of it; heartsick because she knew that nothing in her life would ever compensate her for not having his love.

When she didn't say anything he continued drily, 'But then of course I'm forgetting that making love with me isn't an experience you want to repeat, or so you say. That pride of yours must be a heavy burden to bear at times, Emma. It has to be appeased at all costs hasn't it? No matter what.'

His words forced her into retaliation. 'If you have to believe that quite simply I didn't find your love-making pleasurable enough to want to repeat the exercise, then by all means do so Drake,' she told him, holding her breath as she prayed to be forgiven the enormity of the lie. Her body still ran hot and tremulous now even at the thought of his hands upon it.

'Really? Permit me to tell you that you have the oddest way of signifying your lack of pleasure,' he told her sardonically, 'I have a distinct and very vivid memory of the way you cried my name when you abandoned yourself to me, Emma—and of the way you responded to me. But you aren't ringing me up so that we can discuss old times are you?' he continued smoothly before she could react. 'Very well Emma, I will come to Camilla's dinner party with you. What time do you want me to pick you up?'

She told him seven-thirty and, having thanked him formally for his assistance, hung up.

It was sheer reaction that made her dream of him that night, she told herself on waking; sheer chance that she had woken heavy-eyed and headachy, knowing that she had been crying in her sleep.

Don't be any more of a fool than you already have, she chided herself over breakfast. You're fathoms deep in love with the man; so much so that . . . that the mere thought of seeing him sent her into a tense panic. She could only pray that from somewhere she would find the strength not to betray to him how she felt. Cursing her sister, she finished her cup of coffee and reminded herself that she was here in Cambridge to work— supposedly the most powerful panacea there was.

Hours later, she admitted that either because of the strength of her love or the quality of her job it was a panacea that did not work for her. She could barely go five minutes without thinking about Drake; without aching for him. Fool, fool, she derided herself. Forget him, forget everything about him. But that was far easier said than done.

CHAPTER TEN

SEVEN twenty-five; just five more minutes to go. Emma paced the floor tensely, half of her praying that Drake would arrive soon and the other hoping that he would not. How was she going to live through the evening ahead? How could she, without betraying to him how she felt? You'll find a way, she told herself stoically, reflecting rather wryly that if nothing else, love was a great leveller; her present behaviour was rather more Camilla than Emma.

He arrived at seven-thirty on the dot; the sound of a car drawing up outside and then the door slamming making her stomach nerves clench in on themselves. She wasn't going to the window to look she told herself firmly; fighting against the impulse to rush to the door and open it before he knocked.

Seeing him brought a flood of pain and aching need. She wanted to touch him so badly that not doing so required a positive effort of will. He was dressed formally in a dinner suit, and he looked so urbane and polished that had she seen him like this at their first meeting she might have been deceived into thinking he was simply another smooth dilettante.

Watching him move towards her was an education though; how could she have forgotten that powerful economy of movement; in many ways he reminded her of a jungle predator forced to assume the guise of a domestic cat.

170

'Ready?'

Something glinted in his eyes as she moved towards him, almost in a state of trance. She had agonised for hours over what to wear—very unlike her—wanting to appear at her best and yet anxious not to give him the idea that she had dressed to impress him. In the end she had settled for a simple silk two piece, which was both elegant and restrained. It had also cost her far more than she had intended to spend, but it was worth every penny simply to see the masculine appreciation in his eyes as his glance lingered on her slender shape.

'You've lost weight.'

His observation startled her.

'Have I?' How tense and clipped her voice sounded. She shrugged casually.

'You're not suffering from a broken heart then?'

For a moment her heart almost stopped beating. She forced herself to look at him, determined to withstand the cruelty of his deadly barb and then realised as she met his eyes that his remark had simply been a casual comment. There was no special knowledge or mockery in his eyes as they rested on her pale face; no indication that he knew exactly why she had lost weight; in fact if anything he too looked thinner, Emma reflected, at liberty to study him at close quarters for the first time since his arrival.

'Well?' The harsh grittiness of his voice startled her.

'Well what?' she asked lightly.

Instead of responding he touched her face lightly; holding it so that she couldn't avoid his eyes. The mere brush of his fingers against her skin burned like fire, she wanted to pull away; to retreat before she humiliated herself completely by turning her lips into his palm and betraying exactly what she was suffering from.

'Don't play games with me Emma,' he warned her, his voice still faintly harsh. You know exactly what I mean. Have you actually found a man to whom you can give both your heart and your body?'

He sounded so tauntingly derisive that she was betrayed into immediate retaliation.

'Yes,' she told him simply, forgetting for a moment how much she had to be on her guard against him, and remembering only how he had mocked her for wanting to love and be loved by the man with whom she shared her body.

Her response seemed to throw him slightly. His hand dropped away from her face, a frown creasing his forehead.

'Camilla will be wondering where on earth we are,' Emma said brittly into the tense silence. 'We'd better be on our way.'

'By all means, let's not keep Camilla waiting.'

The tension inside the car was something that could almost be felt, Emma reflected silently, wondering what on earth it was she had said to provoke Drake's almost bitter withdrawal.

It didn't take long to reach the Manor. Camilla greeted them half sullenly; it was almost as though she resented their being there Emma thought in some surprise, which was ridiculous when she remembered that Camilla had been the one to suggest their meeting.

David welcomed her with an awkward hug and a brief kiss, before turning to shake hands with Drake. Her brother-in-law was masking his suspicions well, she thought watching the small inter-change. There were no signs of jealousy or distrust on David's face as he led the way into the drawing-room, and it occurred to Emma that as always her sister could have been guilty of some degree of exaggeration.

On the pretext of offering to help with the meal she left the two men together and followed Camilla into the kitchen. Her sister was talking to Mrs Berry when Emma walked in. She frowned petulantly when she saw Emma.

'Mother isn't at all pleased about tonight,' she told Emma crossly. She wanted us to go out to dinner with her—with some old friends who could help David if he decides to go ahead and enter local politics.'

Who was doing whom the favour here? Emma wondered wryly surveying her sister's flushed and tense face. Stepping out of earshot of Mrs Berry she said coolly, 'Tonight wasn't my idea, Camilla. You were the one who begged me to get in touch with Drake to assuage David's jealousy—re-member?'

'Oh that was only because . . .'

'I can't promise to hold this soufflé for much longer.' Mrs Berry's faintly anxious voice cut in to their conversation.

She would have to try to speak with her sister later on Emma promised herself, heading back to the drawing-room. Camilla was behind her, urging the men to head for the dining-room. Neither of them looked particularly hostile to the other. David was obviously a better actor than she had imagined. Local politics would probably be his metier Emma thought cynically.

A little to her surprise the dinner table conversation flowed quite freely. She had drunk two glasses of wine before she realised that David was pouring her a third. Nervous tension she decided, sneaking a brief glance at Drake, and wishing she hadn't, as he became aware of her scrutiny, his eyes locking with hers. Dark colour burned up under her skin, and she turned away, shivering slightly, becoming aware as she did so that David was launched on one of his favourite hobby horses.

'A woman's place *is* in the home,' Emma heard him saying, 'and there's no getting away from that fact, especially when she has children . . .'

'I'm afraid I can't agree with you.'

Emma was startled to hear Drake speak so categorically. 'Some women work through necessity and would love nothing more than to be at home with their children; other women although excellent mothers, need the stimulation of a career.'

'That's all very well in theory, but would you let your wife work?' David demanded quite heatedly.

'I doubt it would be a question of "allowing".' Drake shrugged his shoulders. 'In my book, a good marriage is a true partnership and if my wife felt the need to have a career independent of me then I would support her in that decision. After all, I would scarcely expect her to demand that I gave up my career or my interests.'

'But if you had children,' Camilla put in, 'surely then you would want their mother to be at home with them.'

'I should *want* it yes,' Drake agreed equably, 'but only if that was what she wanted too.'

'And yet Emma's given up her television career,' David broke in glancing half triumphantly at Drake.

Emma was conscious of three pairs of eyes all focused on her. Drake's responses to David's questions had caused her both pleasure and pain. Pleasure that he could be generous and open-minded enough to give the woman he loved the freedom to make her own choices in life, and pain because she would never be that woman.

Of the three of them only Drake knew the real reason why she had given up her television career, but if she was Drake's wife would she have wanted to continue with it? Facing the question honestly Emma spoke slowly. 'I have to admit that I'm pulled two ways. Half of me would want to devote my time to my husband and family and yet the sense of self-worth one gets from succeeding in something outside that small world can be very important. Perhaps I'll be one of those women who return to a career once the children are teenagers.'

'I hope not.' Drake's firm denial startled her. She looked at him with unguarded eyes for a moment, quickly turning away when she realised what she might be betraying.

'Emma has an excellent brain which I would hate to see atrophy,' Drake spoke succinctly. 'I would very much like to persuade her to work alongside me as my assistant. It can be hellish lonely and vulnerable at the top of a large corporation; and there's nothing like sharing that burden with the person closest to you.'

'Oh I've never believed that a married couple can work together successfully,' David said stuffily.

Emma wasn't really listening to him. She was fighting against a growing tide of emotional havoc. Did Drake really not know what he was doing to her when he talked so evocatively of a future she knew they would not share? How could he know, she reminded herself; she had taken good care to make sure that her love remained a secret from him. More and more she admired and respected him; she liked him as a person; a fellow human being; as well as loving him as a man. It was a combination that would be pretty hard to beat; maybe even impossible. She stared moodily at her half finished meal, startled to tense irritation when David exclaimed, 'My goodness Emma, that's your third glass of wine. No point in asking you if you want a brandy. What's got into you? You're normally very abstemious?'

'Well perhaps tonight I feel like leaping out of my rut,' Emma told him curtly. She did feel quite light headed; more because she had not been eating properly for the last few weeks than because she had consumed three glasses of wine, but it irritated her to be treated like a child and by David of all people, 'and I should like a brandy,' she added, 'a large one.'

By the time they were saying their goodbyes to Camilla and David, Emma was beginning to regret her bravado. She felt distinctly light-headed and wobbly, and she had not had an opportunity to question Camilla further about David's reaction to Drake. In fact as they left she had the distinct impression that Camilla was out of charity with them both, which was ridiculous when they were the ones doing her the favour.

She said as much to Drake as they walked

towards his car, and was surprised by the small grin of amusement he gave her, but she felt too muzzy-headed to question it.

Once she was in her seat with the belt fastened she leaned back and closed her eyes, wishing the earth would not spin in quite such a violent manner.

It was some time later when she opened them, totally disorientated by the thick darkness outside.

'Where are we?' As she asked the question she glanced at her watch and frowned. They had been driving for just over two hours.

'Drake where are we?' she persisted, when he said nothing. 'We've been travelling for over two hours.'

'I'm taking you home with me,' Drake told her calmly, 'I want to talk to you.'

His cool manipulation of events stunned her, rendering her almost speechless. 'But I don't *want* to go home with you,' she managed at last, the alcoholic affects clearing fast as she tried to come to grips with what he was saying.

'Too bad,' he responded laconically, 'because you don't have much choice.'

He was right there, Emma reflected mentally, subsiding back into her seat. And what on earth did he want to talk to her about so urgently that it required this draconian action? Perhaps he wanted to offer her a job? The thought ran through her mind as she remembered the dinner table conversation, but why should Drake offer *her* a job? Perhaps he was still hoping to persuade her into an affair with him? But why should he do that now when he had been content to ignore her for over three weeks?

Emma was still trying to solve that puzzle when Drake drove into a narrow turning. Gravel crunched beneath the car tyres; the dark shapes of bushes lining the drive. He stopped the car in front of a floodlit Tudor farmhouse of rambling proportions, and said drily, 'Home sweet home—out you get Emma. Or would you prefer me to carry you?'

'I can walk.' She managed to inject a certain dignity into her voice, but it was something she was far from feeling. The thought of him touching her body made her shiver with mingled pleasure and dread. Idiot, she derided herself; he doesn't love you; you know that; stop tormenting yourself.

His choice of home half surprised her. She would have expected something more regal and impressive. This half timber, rambling black and white building looked comfortable and welcoming. It wasn't hard to picture it filled with children and dogs. This impression was reinforced when she stepped into the attractive irregular-shaped hallway. The walls glowed soft cream, the exposed beams mellow and dark.

'Please go into the study and make yourself at home,' Drake told her. 'I just want to go upstairs and change. Dinner suits aren't my favourite clothes.' He grimaced faintly as he spoke, tugging impatiently at his bow tie. Emma felt weak with the longing to go up to him and press her lips against his skin. but she managed to suppress it long enough to stumble blindly through the open door he had indicated.

His study was lined with bookshelves; a comfortable, masculine room slightly untidy and obviously well used.

Too tense to sit down she was studying book titles idly when she heard a sharp brief cry. Instantly alarm tingled through her body. She waited to see if the sound was repeated and when everything remained silent she walked back into the hall and called out tentatively, 'Drake, are you all right?'

There was no answer, and reasoning that he must not have heard her Emma called again. Still there was no response. Now a primitive deep rooted anxiety spread through her body, enmeshing and immobilising her reason with pure fear. What had happened to Drake?

Before she knew what she was doing Emma was hurrying upstairs. When she reached the landing she stared about herself, her eyes finally alighting on an open door.

'Drake?' She walked through it tentatively, her throat so tight that her voice was little more than a croaky whisper.

Drake was sitting on a large bed, minus his shirt, the room smelled sharply of masculine cologne.

'I knocked it off the dresser,' he told her briefly and it soaked my shirt. God,' he grimaced slightly, 'This room reeks of it.'

'I think it's quite pleasant.' Emma spoke automatically, all her senses too intent on registering the magnificence of Drake's naked torso, to concentrate on mere speech.

'Do you?' He got up and came towards her reaching her before Emma had time to think properly.

'Heaven help me Emma, but I want you.' His voice was thick, slurred almost, as though *he* had been the one drinking and not her. His fingers punished the feminine sensitivity of her upper arms, the heat coming off his bare skin engulfing her in a tide of sexual awareness that drowned out every other emotion.

'Emma!' He groaned her name, his hands sliding down to her wrists, pinning them behind her back as he bent his head and touched his tongue tentatively against her lips.

Emma tried to strangle an involuntary moan of pleasure that rose to her lips, but they were already parting traitorously, eagerly seeking the tormenting exploration of Drake's tongue.

Time and reality both ceased to exist. They were simply two people bound up in the same spell; bound by a need so intense that no mere human will-power could overset it.

Emma wasn't aware of Drake sliding the clothes from her body; only the delirious relief of feeling his skin against her own as he lifted her on to the bed and joined her there.

'Emma. God you're so beautiful. So perfectly female. I thought I remembered every single thing about you,' Drake muttered rawly, bending over her to stroke long fingers over the curved outline of her body. 'I thought I'd committed every last detail irrevocably to memory, but memories are nothing—starlight to the strength of the sun— when you compare them to the real thing.'

'Starlight is kinder,' Emma responded, the words hard to utter as her senses responded passionately to the intensity with which he was studying her.

'Perhaps in that its failure to mimic the sun helps us to forget what we've lost. My memories didn't do you justice Emma. Nothing could re-create the special silky smoothness of your skin; the way you tremble when I touch you; the way your body responds to mine.'

His mouth silenced the response she would have made, the fierce intensity of his kiss obliterating any ability to think. As she slid her arms round his neck and encountered the male heat of his skin Emma knew she was lost; drowning in water so deep that it was pointless to even think of fighting against its insidious pull.

The lightest brush of his fingers against her skin set off explosive bursts of pleasure so intense that they shook her body, causing Drake to mutter thick words of encouragement and praise as he witnessed her response to his caresses.

Need, anguish, love; all became one fierce torrent of emotion that would not be denied. Her fevered response to him seemed to have a cataclysmic effect on Drake. His mouth burned against her skin; fierce in its possession, the boundaries of his self-control dissolving in the heat of their mutual need.

When Emma arched instinctively beneath him he cried out her name; the male thrust of his body against and within her own so deeply welcomed by her senses that Emma could not conceive how she had existed without him.

Her body starved of his touch and proximity; incited and seduced, betraying instincts Emma hadn't known she possessed. The first time they had made love there had been pleasure it was true, but this ... this total giving of herself ... this heady power of knowing that Drake was as powerless to resist the lure of her body as she was his, seemed to unite them in a way that made them truly equal partners.

'Emma!' She felt Drake tense and tremble slightly against her, his eyes almost black, his skin so hot to the touch that it almost burned.

'Emma, what you do to me.' His body shuddered in release against hers, setting off explosive surges of pleasure that increased in volume until she was crying out his name, relishing the fierce drag of his teeth against her nipple.

Later lying sated and relaxed in Drake's arms it was too much of an effort to move; or to think about what she was doing. Her eyes closed and she curled instinctively into the warmth of Drake's body.

It was light when she woke up; knowing before she opened her eyes that something was wrong; but not knowing what it was. Her body felt pleasantly lethargic; she stretched automatically without opening her eyes, pushing back the bed clothes to uncurl her body with an instinctive sensuality.

'You look exactly as a woman should when she's well and truly been loved.'

Drake's voice jolted her back to instant reality, her body freezing tensely as she reached quickly for the covers. Drake stopped her, the knowledge of his proximity forcing her to open her eyes. Unshaven, he was dressed in a brief bathrobe, his eyes hard and unmerciful as they witnessed her embarrassment.

'What's the matter Emma?' he taunted bitingly, 'Had a sudden attack of conscience? Perhaps that man you've found, isn't the right one after all,' he derided. 'To judge by the way you responded to me last night you haven't found *physical* satisfaction with anyone else.'

'And of course that's all important,' Emma lashed back at him, too confused and hurt by the knowledge that what had happened between them last night was to him, merely the satisfaction of a physical urge, to think about what she was saying.

'It certainly helps,' Drake agreed, 'and don't try telling me that this man you've found can fulfil you sexually Emma, your body tells me a different story. It was starving for me ... *for me!*' he underlined humiliatingly, 'and don't bother trying to deny it . . .'

'I was tipsy,' Emma muttered, turning away from him, desperate for any means of escape. Why oh why had she been betrayed into saying 'Yes' when he asked her if she had found a man whom she loved with her heart and her body? How long could she prevent him from realising just who that man was.

'That's my Emma.' His voice was angry, his eyes hard and cold. 'Make the facts fit her own preconceived ideas. You're not still tipsy this morning I trust?'

Emma shook her head, wanting only to escape from the bed and from him. 'Good, then we'll just put your little theory to the test shall we?' he suggested calmly.

As his meaning hit her she tried to squirm away but he was streets ahead of her, pinning her to the bed with one hand, while the other grasped her hair, forcing her to lie still. Just for a second she felt a tense spiral of fear convulse her body, but the moment Drake's mouth covered her own it was gone, smothered in a long slow surge of pleasure. She tried to fight against it, arching her body, not in invitation but in angry rejection.

'Oh no you don't,' Drake told her thickly, kneeling on the bed beside her, 'I'm going to make you admit how good it is between us even if it takes me all day. In fact I hope it does,' he added with raw emphasis, 'because I'm going to enjoy every single second of it.'

'Sex means nothing without love.' Emma almost cried the words too wrought up by her body's almost instant betrayal to use caution.

'To you? I don't believe that Emma.' Drake's mouth was wry as he studied her flushed face and angry eyes. 'You enjoyed every minute of what we had together last night, but if your memory needs jogging. . .'

The moment his fingers touched her skin Emma knew she was lost. The slow circles he drew round the aching peak of her breast were sheer torment, and although she tried her best to resist him, it was impossible not to move frenziedly against him, inviting the erotic possession of his mouth against her breasts, at first teasing and then arousing her to the point where her body ached tormentingly for the maleness of his.

'*Now* tell me you don't want me.' His voice was thick, heavily slurred, his body as aroused as hers Emma recognised shiveringly when he lifted his head. 'You want me, Emma.'

'Not without love, Drake.' She moved her head from side to side, fighting to deny her love for him and regain some sense of reality. 'Please don't make it harder for me than it already is?'

'Harder for *you*?' Drake swore violently, grasping her wrists and forcing her arms down beside her body. 'Just how the hell do you think I feel, Emma?' he demanded rawly. 'You're tearing my guts out. Believe me if there was some magic spell I could use to make you feel about me the way I feel about you, I'd move heaven and earth to find it. As it is ... Well you can't deny that sexually you're responsive to me ... Let me show you how good it could be for us Emma.'

'And when you're tired of me?' Emma asked achingly. 'I'm not like your other women, Drake, I just couldn't take that.'

'Tired of you?' His voice betrayed an aching pain she had never thought to see in him. 'Dear God, Emma don't you know yet that that will never be. When first you demanded to see me I'll admit I dismissed you without a second thought until it occurred to me that I could use you. And then I saw you——' he smiled in self-derision. 'I wanted you so badly it hurt. When you agreed to pose for the magazine I was glad; glad that you had a flaw. When I found out you'd turned down your job, I knew my first instincts had been right and that not only were you beautiful in body, you were also beautiful in mind and spirit. I had to see you again; to wipe the slate clean and start afresh, but I knew those photographs would always be between us, so I devised a way of blackmailing you into getting engaged to me. I thought if I put on enough pressure, worked hard enough at it, you'd be bound to ...'

'Give in?' Emma supplied wryly. 'Well I did.'

'Yes,' Drake agreed bitterly, 'Have you any idea what it did to me when you thought we were really engaged; when you wanted me as I'd...' He broke off and shook his head wearily. 'I shouldn't have made love to you that night; I knew it at the time and yet I literally couldn't help myself.'

'Why won't you give it a try, Emma? Let me prove to you that we *can* build something that will last on what we have.'

Hiding her surprise Emma studied him. 'I thought long lasting structures were something you made a point of avoiding,' she remarked drily.

'That was before I fell in love with you.'

He said it so simply that for a moment she couldn't speak, and then her opportunity to do so was gone as Drake continued urgently, 'This other man Emma, whoever he is, I don't believe you really love him. I know you. You'd never have responded to me the way you did if that were the case. I don't know who he is but . . .'

'On the contrary,' Emma interrupted coolly, fighting down a rising tide of pure, intense joy, 'you know him very well. It's you Drake,' she told him when he simply watched her. 'I love you.'

His instant withdrawal from her was not what she had expected. He half turned away from her as he said thickly, 'Emma if this is some sort of act of pity, forget it. I can take the fact that you don't love me, because I believe we can build a lasting marriage on what we have, but what I don't want are false promises; false hopes.'

'Drake.' She reached up cupping his face with her hands, smiling tremulously into his eyes. 'It's no act, and the only person I'm likely to pity is myself, because I've been through agony loving you and believing that you merely wanted me. When I talked about wanting love and desire I was talking about my wanting of your love as well as your desire.'

'I thought you meant that while you desired me physcially you didn't love me. In fact you said as much.'

'Because I was frightened that you'd guess the truth and that you'd use it to urge me into a relationship which ultimately could only cause me pain.'

'It's a very high opinion you have of me,' he murmured sardonically, 'but perhaps well deserved. If you marry me Emma, it will be for life . . .'

She smiled mischieviously at him. 'I shouldn't want it any other way.' He paused bending his head to kiss her. Against her body Emma could feel the deep, rapid thud of his heart. He loved her . . . Drake loved her . . . The knowledge pierced thrillingly through her.

'Just think,' she said dreamily as he lowered her back against the bed. 'If it hadn't been for David being suspicious of you and Camilla insisting on that dinner party we might never have learned the truth.'

Drake paused, removing his robe. The morning sunlight gleamed rich bronze on his body and Emma couldn't resist lifting her hand to stroke the satin smoothness of his skin. The ripple of pleasure that surged through him made her tremble in immediate response, but she froze in tense dread as Drake said quietly, 'I'm afraid I have a confession to make.'

What was he going to tell her? That his proclamation of love had been a trick all along? No, she didn't believe he could be so cruel.

'I coerced Camilla into going to you with that tale, by threatening to tell David about the night she spent at my house—with suitable embellishments of course. Naturally, I wouldn't have done so, but it was enough to make her come running to you, and to make you, with true sisterly loyalty come to me. You see I knew if I approached you, you'd run away from me and I was desperate for the sight and touch of you, Emma. I told myself that somehow we'd talk but it just didn't work out that way. First you dropped your bombshell about finding someone you loved. I was almost mad with jealousy. I couldn't believe you could love someone else and yet have reacted so passionately to me. I told myself if I could just get you into bed; break down the barriers you had erected between us I could make you see that there was only one man for you—me. Hence the spilled cologne . . . I hoped my crying out might bring you upstairs . . .'

'Lazy beast,' Emma derided, 'after all the least I might have expected was to be swept up in your arms and carried off in true romantic fashion.'

'Umm, knowing you, you'd have kicked and fought all the way,' Drake told her. 'No, I knew I had to catch you off-guard . . . to break down the barriers you'd put up against me.'

'Well you certainly succeeded in that.' She coloured faintly, remembering her abandoned response to his lovemaking.

'Umm, maybe, but you're not leaving this bed until I have your promise that you'll marry me.'

'You mean you'll trust my word?' Emma teased, rounding her eyes in mock amazement. 'Don't you know you should never believe anything someone says in the throes of passion?'

Drake shook his head. 'Wrong,' he said softly. 'When passion is combined with love, it's stronger than any truth serum ever invented. Last night it took every ounce of self control I had not to tell you how much I loved and needed you. You were right Emma,' he told her huskily, 'sex without love is a mere shadow of the real thing. Tell me you love me,' he demanded rawly. 'Let me hear you say it.'

Intuitive to his deep-rooted need to be sure of her Emma whispered the words against his ear. She also murmured them against his throat reinforcing them with soft kisses. She was still murmuring them as her tongue touched the flat plane of his belly, but it seemed Drake had heard them enough. 'Now tell me that you'll marry me,' he commanded thickly.

Emma needed no second bidding, but she continued to tease him with light kisses and caresses for several seconds before she did so, caught off guard by Drake's sudden transition from supplicant to aggressor as he rolled her away from his body and then began to tease and torment her as she had been doing him.

Quite when teasing gave way to passion Emma didn't know, she only knew that her body welcomed the surge of Drake's against it as though it had been fashioned just for it, the words of love he muttered into her skin finding a feverish response within her. Drake loved her. There was nothing more she asked from life. She already had it all safely encompassed within the confines of this bed; held fast to her with arms she knew would never let her go. Later they would talk and plan, right now was the time to feel and to share those feelings; to give and receive life's most precious gift of all. That of love.